little girl unknown

The Cherrystone Creek Mysteries: Book 1

Emma Jackson

All Rights Reserved. Copyright © 2020
Smith Beach Press

This is a work of fiction. Any resemblance to actual persons, living or dead, are purely happenstance. The names used in the book are composites of names common to the area, to assure verisimilitude. All rights reserved, including the right to reproduce this book, or portions thereof, in any form. No part of this text may be reproduced, transmitted, downloaded, decompiled, reverse engineered, or stored in or introduced into any information storage and retrieval system, in any form or by any means, whether electronic or mechanical without the express written permission of the author. The scanning, uploading, and distribution of this book via the Internet or via any other means without the permission of the author is illegal and punishable by law. Please purchase only authorized electronic editions, and do not participate in or encourage electronic piracy of copyrighted materials.

Editing by Debbie Maxwell Allen
Cover by Shayne Rutherford
Dark Moon Graphics

Interior Design by Colleen Sheehan
Ampersand Book Designs
Back Cover and Amazon Blurbs by Shelley Ring

Smith Beach Press

SMITHBEACHPRESS.COM

ISBN-13: 978-1-7338928-5-8

Preface

THE EASTERN SHORE of Virginia is a real place. A wonderful place. If you want to read some more about it try AN EASTERN SHORE SKETCHBOOK by David Thatcher Wilson available on Amazon. Additionally, Cape Charles, Eastville, and Northampton County are real. Donna Bozza, mentioned in the book, is the Executive Director of the Citizens For A Better Eastern Shore, a group dedicated to saving the Eastern Shore from polluters, developers, and other n'er do wells. Yuk Yuk and Joe's is real, as are Machipongo Trading Company, Rayfield's and Cape Charles Coffee House. Most of the names in the book are amalgamations of the names of people from the Eastern Shore of Virginia (ESVA). I felt that using Shore-common surnames like Kellam, Smith, Goffigon, Heath and others would add some verisimilitude to my story. They are not based on any real people, living or dead. Just borrowed the surnames.

Come visit our website

Smith Beach Press

SMITHBEACHPRESS.COM

Prologue

CHERRYSTONE INLET IS a quiet tributary. Branching off of the southern reaches of the Chesapeake Bay, probing into Virginia's Eastern Shore (ESVA), it is a favorite hunting ground for the Great Blue Heron searching for crabs and high-soaring Osprey searching for small fish. Raccoons, too, are there and the occasional playful otter. At the mouth of the creek there is a commercial campground, Cherrystone Family Camping Resort, but up past Mill Point there's nothing but farmland and some stands of mostly pine trees. The water is fairly shallow with snags and eelgrass for the crabs to hide in. It's peaceful and bucolic, a perfect place to explore with a shallow-draft boat.

It was dark as the small craft silently glided up the creek. No one saw the small craft pass with its small cargo bundled up front. The paddler waited until there were no farmhouses visible on the wooded bank and carefully eased the bundle from the bow of the vessel into the water, where it quickly sank to the bottom. There the body of the little girl unknown lay in quiet repose, snugly wrapped in an old piece of fishnet, a feast for the crabs, weighted down with broken chunks of concrete block in just a few feet of brackish water. The boat melted back into the quiet dark.

Chapter One

AT 6:30 AM the clock radio softly clicked on and WESR-AM, the only radio station she could reliably get, started reporting the day's local weather, marine weather, and local and national news. Not wanting to yield to being awake, Paige rolled over and pulled the pillow over her head to try for just another fifteen minutes of sleep. She was peacefully drifting when—oomph! Her eighteen-pound male Maine Coon Cat Pongo, feeling that it was time for Paige to get up and feed him, leaped off the dresser and into the middle of her back. Shocked into full wakefulness Paige reached for David Wilson's AN EASTERN SHORE SKETCHBOOK from her nightstand and threw it at the swiftly retreating feline.

"Blast you, Pongo!" she cried. But the large green-eyed cat merely gazed at her impassively from the hallway outside her door, as he studiously licked his right paw. He knew it was time to get up, even if his mistress didn't. Paige had found Pongo as a cute little stray kitten next to a trash pile behind Machipongo Trading Company when she stopped for breakfast one morning. She had no idea he would grow so large or that his strong personality would end up running her homelife. She might have left him there. But those green eyes!

Throwing her bedding on the floor Paige stomped to the bathroom, slamming the door behind her. As she let the electric toothbrush do its thing, she closed her eyes and said a quick prayer for her day. *Dear Lord, thank you for bringing me safely to this new day. Please bless whatever it is you have in store for me today and let me be a good representative for You. Thanks. Amen.* She scrubbed her face with a piece of loofah until her skin fairly glowed. She used very little makeup. She didn't need to. As Paige brushed out her strawberry blond hair Pongo came into the bathroom and rubbed up against her legs purring.

"That's not going to get you any forgiveness," she said. "All I wanted was ten more minutes. All you wanted was to fill your belly."

Nonplussed the cat looked up at her again, then nonchalantly wandered down the hall to the apartment's little kitchen.

Paige dressed in a calf-length khaki skirt, a long-sleeved crisply starched blue denim shirt and brown knee-high leather boots, her "office uniform," as she called it. She fed Pongo, not making anything for herself, hopped in her car and headed down the road to Cape Charles.

Got to press the flesh and keep prospective clients happy, she thought. *And getting my morning fix of latte and a pastry and some gossip is a must, too.*

Paige had been well-known and well-liked in her days at Northampton High School and having Big Bill Reese, the glad-handing local undertaker as her daddy helped a lot. That was lucky, now that she was back home. Running a successful undertaking business required an excellent relationship with the people in the county. She enjoyed visiting and gossiping with the folks down in Cape Charles and Eastville, and in church up in Foxtown, and her daily routine was based on that.

Most days started with breakfast at Cape Charles Coffee House with Roberta's great baked goods and talk with her closest friend, Donna. The building the Coffee House occupied was once the Cape Charles Bank, built in 1910. When they renovated, they did so with style, keeping the decorative pressed tin ceiling, the intricately carved moldings, the art deco chandeliers, and the second-floor gallery. It was a delightful place to visit and breakfast.

Lunch was at Machipongo Trading Company or Yuk Yuk and Joe's, often with her friend Pam Kellam, the Eastville postmistress, or Ann Webster Goffigon, the Clerk of Court. For dinner she would usually go to Cove Restaurant at Mallard Cove Marina south of Cape Charles, or sometimes enjoy sunset drinks at The Jackspot on the bayside of the tip of the peninsula. The southern point of the Eastern Shore, Northampton County, was a small enough community that Paige was always going to run into folks she knew in all these places, and unless she was very unlucky, she'd often get someone else to pick up her tab.

This morning it only took Paige about fifteen minutes to get to the Coffee House. She parked on the street, with its strange back-in diagonal parking, and as she walked in the door her senses were assaulted by the intoxicating smells of espresso and fresh baked goods.

Her mouth immediately began to water as she headed to the left side, where a small table was flanked by two huge overstuffed wing chairs. Her good friend Donna Bozza, the Executive Director of CBES, Citizens for a Better Eastern Shore, was already seated and drinking a foamy cappuccino.

"Paige," called Donna, waving her over. Blonde Donna looked like a beach girl, dressed in casual clothes her hair carefully wind-tossed, her smooth skin tanned. She was a "come here," a Yankee who had moved down and stayed, so her accent wasn't pure, but no one really minded that anymore. She was a valuable addition to the area.

As Paige headed toward the table, she waved to Roberta at the espresso machine. "The usual?" called Roberta, and Paige nodded.

The usual was a large latte with a freshly baked still warm cranberry muffin.

Paige and Donna chatted over their breakfasts. Donna was planning for the annual fund raising Between The Waters Bike Tour and hoping to get some corporate support from Reese Funeral Industries and Cape Charles Coffee House. Proudly she showed Paige the colorful poster she had commissioned for the event from a local artist. "And we'll hold a raffle for the original painting," she enthused. She hoped that she could count on Paige's help with the organization of the event. Paige was always anxious and willing to help.

Paige and Donna nibbled and drank and talked until Donna, glancing out the front window, said, "There he goes."

Paige turned and looked out the window. Across Mason Avenue painfully limped a figure of indeterminate age. It was a male, that could be seen. He wore a gray t-shirt, desert camo pants tucked into filthy white rubber waterman's boots, and a greasy green ball cap from which long straggling brown hair hung down to his shoulders.

"Who's that?" Paige asked.

"Nott Smith," Donna replied smiling grimly and shaking her head. "Our resident hermit."

"I don't think I've ever seen him before," said Paige. "Tell me about him."

"I don't know much ... just that he was in the war and has some problems left over from it."

THE PREVIOUS NIGHT

FLASH! THE INTENSE *light lanced through Nott's closed eyelids, through his deep sleep, and into the fight-flight portion of the brain that tells a person they are in trouble. He began* *struggling up from the depths of his dreams into a feeling of unnamed dread.* BOOM! *The bed Nott was sleeping on shook violently with the concussion. His eyes popped open though they were focused elsewhere on an unseen world of his own.*

Incoming mortars! *his mind screamed.*

Nott reached for his M4 carbine as he rolled off his bunk to the floor. Where is that damn rifle? he thought. He gave up scrabbling for it in the dark and tried frantically to burrow down into the splintery wooden floor, making himself as small as possible. The rattle of small arms fire filled his ears and caused him to hunker down even farther. He lay curled in a tight ball, virtually catatonic, until the morning sun shone brightly into his face through a crack in the wall.

Waking and looking around Nott found himself lying partly under his scrounged canvas camp cot, tangled up in the quilted desert camouflage poncho liner he used for his only bedding. He untangled himself, stood and looked out the window at the marshland surrounding the shack, his home. The bright day belied the thunder and hail of the night before, the only sign of it being the several inches of water in the bottom of Nott's boat.

Chapter Two

NOTT
1985

WHEN MOLLY SMITH'S water broke it was after three o'clock on a hot August morning. Her husband, Jimbo, was passed-out drunk, as usual, and didn't even hear the screams as her labor cramps got worse. Not that he would have been of any help. The only things he could do were pick vegetables and drink, though not necessarily in that order or independent of each other.

Their migrant shack in Machipongo had electricity and running water, but the sanitary facilities were a small smelly hut out back and a telephone was not in their non-existent budget. It didn't matter. She didn't have a doctor, anyway. Her screams did bring Lupe, the *curandera,* or Mexican medicine woman. Molly was glad Jimbo was passed out. He hated Lupe and all the other Mexican migrant workers who lived in their little shantytown. It was one of the reasons he drank—to forget that he was of a like social status with these ... wetbacks.

Lupe stayed by Molly's side, wiping the sweat from her forehead, speaking soft words of encouragement, and giving her ice chips and an herbal tea that she had brewed from plants she found in the woods and byways. It had a calming effect although, admittedly, it did little to ease Molly's pain.

After five hours of this Jimbo groggily woke up. Seeing Lupe, he cried out, "What's that witch doing here?" He was struggling to his feet to throw her out when another vicious contraction made Molly shriek in pain and startled Jimbo so much that he fell back onto the sofa.

"What are you doing to her?" he cried.

"Helping her birth her baby," Lupe replied. "If you do not want me here, I'll leave, and you can do it." Molly moaned.

Finally making it to his feet Jimbo grabbed his bottle and lurched out the door of the shack. Lupe gave a little satisfied smile. "Here you go, *cariña.* Drink some more of my tea and it will help the baby come."

Squatting between Molly's knees, Lupe lifted the edge of her dress. "You will push hard with the next cramp."

Molly gasped in a deep breath and with the next contraction she held her breath and pushed as though she was trying to expel a watermelon.

"Push," encouraged Lupe and Molly groaned.

Suddenly, with a swish and a squish, the baby was there. Lupe quickly wiped the mucus out of the baby's mouth and gently put him to Molly's breast. "It is a beautiful boy," she told Molly. "And he is perfect."

Craning her head Molly looked down at the little red *thing* that was glommed onto her breast, sucking like he had never eaten before. "He's beautiful," she breathed, as her head sank back on the pillow. "*Gracias,* Lupe."

"*Por nada,* little one," the old woman said and moved to clean up the bloody bedclothes.

The baby was named James, after his daddy. And since they were picking tomatoes on the Nottingham farm, he became James Nottingham Smith. His mama called him "Nott."

As a kid, Nott never realized how poor they were. Oh, he'd sometimes see the Nottingham kids riding shiny bicycles or riding in little pony-drawn carts, but all the kids who lived close to him, the many Mexican kids living there in the migrant camp, had just as much, or as little, as he did. And it wasn't bad growing up on the rural Eastern Shore of Virginia. When he wasn't in the field helping his parents he could fish, he could wade in the shallows over on seaside and rooch his toes in the mud looking for clams. Why on a good day he could bring home a dozen or more.

Sometimes he'd borrow a dip net and go crabbing. He'd put an old bushel basket in an inner tube and tie a cord from it to his waist, and then sneak through the eel-grass in the shallows watching for blue crabs. He'd quickly but gently scoop them up in his net, then just as quickly flip the net upside down over his basket to shake the crab out before it got itself tangled up in the net. If he wasn't fast enough, then he'd have to carefully untangle the crab while looking out for its powerful claws. He liked crabbing. It seemed fair to him—the crab wanted to get him as much as he wanted to get the crab. He usually won.

During the winter months, when hunting season was on them, Jimbo would go deer hunting. There were so many white-tailed deer on the farm that it was rare for him to not come home with a buck, and the venison kept them in red meat. That and the vegetables they managed to cull while picking meant that they never went hungry, and the fact that they had almost no money didn't affect their bellies. Of course, when they did get some money, Jimbo spent it on cheap whiskey, so it was good that they could provide for their own larder.

It wasn't all roses, though. When Jimbo got drunk, which was much of the time, he seemed to blame Nott for everything. There might not even be anything wrong, but Jimbo would still haul off and take a strap to Nott. Of course, Nott didn't like it, but he was perceptive enough to see that if Jimbo didn't hit him, he'd hit his mama. So, Nott took it to protect her from Jimbo's drunken rages.

And there was nothing they could do about it. Oh, the social worker would occasionally come by from The Shore Labor Health Center, but they couldn't complain to her. If she told the sheriff they'd probably haul Jimbo off, and then they wouldn't have what little income or food he brought in. Besides, it wasn't anyone's business but their own. They didn't need outsiders interfering with their lives. This was just the way life was.

The older Nott got, however, the harder it was for him to just stand there and let Jimbo beat on him. He probably could have taken the old man in a fight, especially when he was in one of his drunken rages and stumbling around, but then where would they be? Jimbo would leave them, and they'd be alone.

The breaking point came on Nott's sixteenth birthday. He didn't receive any presents. He didn't expect to. But Jimbo declared now that Nott was a man, he, Jimbo, didn't see why he should support him anymore. Drunk, as usual, he gave Nott twenty-four hours to move out of the shack. Molly cried and protested the loss of her only child, but Jimbo was adamant. Nott had to go.

This was fine by Nott. He was tired of the beatings and he was tired of his father's drunken rages. He hated to leave his mama, but he knew he had to. She cried and clung to him, but he gently rubbed her back and promised that he'd be all right and that he'd let her know where he ended up. He told her that he was going to make a lot of money and when he did, he was coming back for her. The dreams of a sixteen-year-old.

Nott didn't own much more than the clothes on his back, but early the next morning, while Jimbo was still sleeping off the previous night's bender, Nott kissed his mama goodbye and walked out to Route 13 to hitchhike out of there. He wasn't certain where he wanted to go, but he wanted it to be far away from the Machipongo Migrant Camp and his drunken daddy. The highway was just three lanes wide, one lane going each direction and a passing lane in the middle, so Nott stood in the middle lane and stuck his thumb out for traffic going both directions, north and south.

It only took about an hour until a rattletrap pickup truck headed north pulled onto the shoulder of the road and waited for Nott to catch up.

The driver was a black man, old and dusty with years of toil etched into the crags of his face. "Where ya goin', boy?" he asked.

"Uh, north," answered Nott.

"Any place in particular or jes' north?"

Good question and Nott didn't have a good answer. "Just north, I guess."

"You runnin' from sommat? Y'ain't got the laws after you, has you?"

"No, no one's after me. I'm just travelin'," answered Nott and sat looking out the window at the fields passing by.

"Um hm," said the old black man, and they drove on in silence.

As they approached Onancock the silence was getting oppressive. "I gots a grandson 'bout your age," said the old man. "What's really up wit' ya?"

Nott didn't like spilling his guts to someone he didn't know, but the old man seemed kind and genuine, so he told him about how his daddy was a drunk who beat him and how for a sixteenth birthday present he had thrown him out of the house.

"Hmmm," the old man said. "So, what ya gonna do? Where ya gonna go?"

"I don't know," said Nott. "I'm just gonna see what happens."

"No, that jes won't do. We gots to have a plan of some sorts. Ya ever think about the Army?"

"I'm only sixteen. And there's no way I can get my parents to sign for me."

The old man was quiet for a while.

"Tell you what. I was only goin' far as Accomac. But if ya want, I'll drive ya all the way to the Army Recruitin' Office in Salisbury."

"But I'm only sixteen," Nott protested.

"Listen, boy. I spent twenty-two years in the green machine. Best years of my life. They'll grow you up. They'll teach you a trade. Ya get three squares a day and a place to sleep and clothes. You ever been off 'The Shore'?"

Nott shook his head.

"Didn' think so. Shoot. You got nothin' to keep you here. Army'll get you away, get you trained, and if you like it like I did it's a good place to stay."

"What did you do in the Army?" asked Nott.

"I was a 88-mike, a truck driver. But you can do whatever you want. And the girls love guys in uniform."

"I'm only sixteen!"

"Tell you what. Here's what we do. Tell them you're seventeen. If they don't buy it and want somethin' signed by a parent, bring it out to me in the truck. I'll sign it. 'Kay?"

The Army recruiter must have been behind in his monthly quota. Nott was hustled through a medical exam, qualification testing, signing and swearing, and by the weekend Nott was in Basic Training at Fort Dix, New Jersey.

Nott did well in basic training. He was in good physical condition from working long days in the fields, and he surprised himself with how well he did in the various classes he had to take. He was able to write to mama, and she wrote back once. She was so proud. She wanted so badly to be there for his graduation, but daddy wouldn't give her the money for bus fare. Nott had been sending her a regular allotment from his pay, but daddy took it as soon as it arrived. He sent her a picture of himself in his uniform, knowing that she would tack it to the wall of the kitchen.

It was after basic training that Nott came to understand the perfidy of some Army recruiters. Nott had told the recruiter that he wasn't sure what he wanted to do in the Army other than learn a trade. The recruiter told him that the bedrock basis of everything in the Army was eleven-bravo, infantry, and after graduation at Ft. Dix Nott found himself on a bus to Ft. Benning, Georgia, for twenty-six weeks of Advanced Infantry Training. This was why, when he ultimately found himself in the Iraq war, it was as a regular soldier, and why he was driving a Humvee when it hit an improvised explosive device.

It was 2006, during the early stages of the Battle of Ramadi. He was driving a dirt road that he had driven several times before when it happened. The sun was out, his gunner was standing in the turret behind him keeping watch for any *unfriendlies*, and the deuce-and-a-half he was escorting was close on his bumper. They'd had no intel about any troubles in the area, and Nott was feeling like it was just a pleasant, though hot, afternoon drive. Until it happened. Afterward he didn't remember hearing any explosion, but he did remember seeing the dirt under the front of his Humvee rising like a bursting bubble, taking the vehicle with it and flipping it aside like a toy. He didn't remember anything after that until he awoke in a field hospital, groggily aware that his entire body felt like he'd been beaten with a baseball bat.

When he was better able to understand the doctors told him what had happened. They assured him that he was alive and would be fine and that he had lost no appendages. Then they told Nott that the explosion had virtually destroyed his legs, that it had only been heroic work by the surgeons that had saved them, but that he'd be getting a disability discharge from the Army as soon as he was judged sufficiently healed. "Look at the bright side," they said, "you'll be going home."

Going home, thought Nott. *I wonder where that is and what I'll do there.* His mama had disappeared while he was in the Army and it was a cinch he wasn't going back to the labor camp, he had two legs that only sort-of worked, and he had no marketable skills. *Going home. Whoopee.*

Chapter Three

PAIGE WASN'T TOO happy about returning to the Eastern Shore either. She started her life back in Eastville feeling resentful and sorry for herself. She had planned her career arc so perfectly—a business degree from William and Mary in Williamsburg, graduate studies in finance at the Wharton School in Philadelphia, and then on to a position of responsibility commensurate with her education and abilities with a large New York corporation where she would eventually become the Chief Financial Officer. *Then daddy had his stroke, Billy was too dumb to cope, and I had to leave Wharton to run Reese Funeral Home. Darn!* she thought.

Luckily brother Billy had gone to the Pittsburgh Institute of Mortuary Science (PIMS) some time ago, so the business was able to run under his license and credentials. But Paige couldn't trust Billy even to be around, so she managed to earn an Associate Degree in mortuary science from PIMS mostly online. Once she finished those studies, because she enjoyed learning and because she found some of the working with dead bodies fascinating, she continued studying online with the Death Investigation Academy and ended up as a Certified Medicolegal Death Investigator. Paige knew that there was no longer a need for a full-blown coroner in Eastville, but she also knew that anything that could be done to help the sheriff would be welcome and would help cement good relations between Reese Funeral Home and the people of Northampton County. Plus, it occasionally gave her the opportunity to work with some of the more eligible bachelors available—the lawyers.

I guess I'm sort of the unofficial coroner. That's fine by me. There's really not a lot of coroner work to do and that there is, is kinda interesting. Plus, it keeps me on really good terms with the Sheriff and CCPD. It's kinda cool, too, how it freaks people out. I guess if I were a girlie-girl I'd have trouble with it but dealing with dead bodies is no big deal. Heck, lots of these people are a lot nicer dead than they ever were to me when they were living.

There wasn't a lot of nightlife in Northampton County. Certainly not what Paige had gotten used to enjoying in Philadelphia. She liked clubbing and dancing, but to do that here she'd have to travel across The Bay to Norfolk or Virginia Beach, and unless she was desperate, it just wasn't worth it. Besides, all the clubs over there were packed with young kids from the Norfolk Naval Base, Little Creek and the other military installations, and it just wasn't her dream to date these pimply-faced over-testosteroned kids.

On occasion, Sheriff's Chief Deputy Pablo Gerena would take Paige to the Cove Restaurant at the newly renovated Mallard Cove Marina. The food was good, and the company was interesting, but Pablo wanted more than Paige was willing to give him. She was pretty sure he wasn't looking for a permanent relationship. He just wanted to get her into bed, and as tempting as it was with Pablo's rock-hard body and smoldering dark Hispanic looks, she just wasn't interested. Paige wasn't looking for a "friends-with-benefits" relationship. If she was going to get that involved, she wanted a probability of permanence.

Pablo had a fast boat that he had acquired in a DEA auction. It was a 38' Cigarette boat, bright yellow with red lightning bolts painted down the sides. He loved that boat more than life itself, and on nice days when he wasn't on duty, he could be seen, and heard, racing up and across The Bay.

Sometimes Pablo would take Paige out for a ride in his boat. She was glad that he didn't like fishing. That would have been just too common for her. Daddy had taken her fishing a couple of times, but he had always insisted that she bait her own hooks and take off any fish that she caught, and it had grossed her out. Paige thought that fish were wonderful, as long as they were breaded and fried or sautéed or baked. She didn't want to be the one to catch them. Fortunately, the fish served at the marina restaurant was generally fresh caught, purchased from one or more of the boats in the charter fleet at the marina.

But Pablo wasn't into fishing, either. He was into speed. Paige didn't know a lot about boats, but Pablo kept telling her that his was probably the fastest boat on the Eastern Shore. He assured her that his boat would go over eighty miles-per-hour. Paige loved the speed and loved how everyone looked at them when they roared by in the flashy go-fast. Even the tourists on the fishing pier at the island of the Chesapeake Bay Bridge-Tunnel would point at them as they flew past, a ten-foot rooster tail sparkling behind them. What she didn't like was how Pablo kept trying to get her to go down into the cabin with him. There was a Porta-Potti in the cabin, and she had visited that when they stayed out too long and bounced over too many waves for her poor bladder to handle, but Pablo wanted her to try out the soft leather upholstered benches that stretched down each side of the cabin. She demurred. He never tried to force her, but she could see the resentment in his face every time it happened.

Chapter Four

AFTER MONTHS IN military hospitals in Iraq, Germany and Washington, numerous operations and sessions of physical therapy and counseling, Nott was medically discharged from the Army. He not only suffered from the damage to his legs, but he also had a severe case of Post-Traumatic Stress Disorder, PTSD. Loud explosions or certain smells, like that of hospital disinfectant or burnt explosives, could quickly send his mind back to combat mode or into a coma-like state. The VA rated his combined disabilities at 100%.

He had lost track of his mama, she had moved away and never written to him to tell him where, so upon discharge, Nott returned to The Shore, the only civilian life he'd ever known, where he lived almost a hermit's life. At first, he slept on the beach at Cape Charles. There was a sculpture of the word LOVE at the beach, and he tried to snuggle up in its shadow in hopes that he'd be less obvious to any of the town cops on patrol. As long as he was up and out early, he could usually get a decent night's rest. When it rained, he would try to hide in the cupola by the street, and if the cops saw him there, they usually just let him go. Cape Charles was a small town and Nott was a known local character. He wasn't considered a war hero, but he was understood to be another homeless veteran who caused no trouble.

During the day Nott just limped painfully around—far and wide. His legs weren't what they were when he was a field hand, but they were strong enough for him to be mobile. He never wore short pants or a bathing suit because he was ashamed of the livid scars left from his many surgeries after being blown up. But at least he could still walk, in his own fashion.

Nott liked exploring the deserted beach of the Cape Charles Natural Preserve south of the harbor. It was a good place to look for useful flotsam washed ashore by storms. Sometimes, when he knew there'd be no rain, Nott would camp in the Preserve. He wasn't supposed to, but again, people knew who he was and if he wasn't causing trouble, they tended to leave him alone.

One day, wandering the deserted beach after a strong storm, Nott found a boat washed up. It wasn't much, just a twelve-foot scow, a work boat with a plugged hole drilled in the bottom to allow it to be washed out. It had been neglected for a good while and the paint was flaking off in sheets. There were no registration numbers on the bow, so Nott took ownership. By brute force he hauled the boat out of the water and up into the woods behind the beach where he could both work on it, and use it for shelter, crawling under it in rainstorms.

Because of his disability, Nott received a monthly stipend from the Veteran's Administration. Not having a permanent address or a bank account, the check was mailed to him monthly at General Delivery at the Cape Charles Post Office. Most months Nott didn't even pick up the check, and when he finally did need some cash, he would only take one of the checks, leaving the others at the post office. It sort of acted his bank. They weren't supposed to, but again, Cape Charles is a small town and tries to take care of its own.

So it was that Nott was able to go to Watson's Hardware on Mason Avenue and pick up the tools and supplies he'd need to fix his boat. Some brass screws, a few tools, some caulking, and paint—it wasn't going to make it new, but it was going to make it serviceable, and that's what he needed.

When he was sleeping on the city beach Nott had gotten into the habit of walking to Rayfield's Pharmacy each morning for coffee. He had to pass the Cape Charles Coffee House to get there, but that place was too fancy for him. Although he did have enough income from the Veterans Administration to afford a latte or cappuccino, Nott was satisfied with just plain, hot, black coffee sitting at the lunch counter at Rayfield's. Birdie, the morning clerk *cum* fountain person took a motherly interest in Nott, and a lot of times she wouldn't even charge him for the coffee or a pastry. In fact, if young Mr. Rayfield wasn't in the store, she'd sometimes fix Nott an entire breakfast of bacon, eggs, grits, biscuits, and gravy. Nott honestly appreciated Birdie's charity, but seldom did more than grunt his appreciation at her. He didn't talk much.

One morning, while opening the door to go into Rayfield's, a passing junker of a pickup truck, smoke billowing from its tailpipe, backfired loudly as it made the turn onto Mason Street. Nott's PTSD kicked in and he dove into the bushes forming a hedge in front of the store. This time he quickly realized what had happened, and as he extricated himself, he looked around furtively to see if anyone had seen his action. Nott was ashamed of his PTSD and figured people would see him as stranger than they already did.

No one outside saw his dive to safety, but Birdie did. She didn't say anything, but she had his coffee ready for him when he sat down and his huge breakfast on the grill. As he bowed his head in a silent grace before eating, he'd always thank God for the food and for Birdie. She never knew. Birdie tried to draw him out and get him to talk, but she knew his story, she'd been in Cape Charles forever, so she didn't try to intrude on his privacy. He was one of "her boys" who had gone off to war and come home broken, and she'd look after him as best she could in her limited ways.

It was a simple and solitary life for Nott. But that left him plenty of time to fix up his boat. While he worked, he kept his eyes open for a small outboard motor. He didn't want anything big. Just enough to push himself around in the creeks off The Bay around Cape Charles. Birdie kept her eyes open, too, and she was able to find a small twelve horsepower Evinrude for only a few hundred dollars. It was in the shed of a friend and only needed a tune-up and the fuel filter replaced. Nott quickly had it running with parts from Cape Charles Marine out on the highway.

Nott was now nautically mobile, though he didn't really have any place to go. He took to exploring, puttering to other stretches of deserted beach south of Cape Charles. He became a beachcomber, sleeping wherever darkness found him.

On one of his excursions, Nott motored north of Cape Charles, past King's Creek and into Cherrystone Inlet. Cruising up the creek Nott found what was going to be his new home—an Oyster Watch House. During the late 1800s what were then called "oyster pirates" were all over the Chesapeake, stealing market-size oysters from other people's oyster beds and selling them to restaurants in Baltimore. To fight the pirates the oyster-raising watermen-built watch houses on stilts over their oyster beds and kept them manned and armed around the clock. They weren't in use anymore, but it was one of these houses, rickety and dilapidated, that Nott found deserted up Cherrystone Creek. He moved in.

Nott's house had cracks in the walls big enough to throw a cat through and a roof that leaked like a sieve, but it was his. Taking some of his VA money he again bought supplies from Watson's Hardware and started fixing the place up. Whenever possible, though, Nott used things that he had scrounged through his beachcombing instead of spending his money.

The shack had no amenities, but Nott had found an Origo non-pressurized alcohol stove on a wrecked sailboat. It only had one burner, but since Nott ate mostly soup, beans, fish and crabs that he caught, it was all he needed. For light, he found a Uco candle lantern. He bought matches at Watson's, but when his candle supply grew low and he got desperate he was known to "borrow" votive candles from St. Charles Roman Catholic Church in Cape Charles.

Nott tried sleeping on the splintery floor of the shack but finally took some of his money and purchased an Army surplus canvas camp cot and a desert camouflage poncho liner from Watson's. That made his home.

When the Virginia Marine Resources Commission passed a law requiring all crab pots to have two cull rings to allow undersized crabs to escape, many commercial crabbers discarded their oldest and most decrepit pots and bought compliant new ones. Nott managed to salvage eight of the old pots which he fixed for his own use. He'd fish with a handline from his boat or from his shack, and use the heads, tails, and guts of the fish he caught for bait as he put out a line of crab pots on up the creek. It was a lonely existence, but between his fish and crabs, morning coffee at Rayfield's and an occasional store-bought can of Dinty Moore stew, Nott was satisfied.

Chapter Five

NOTT WAS SITTING at the counter with his breakfast at Rayfield's. It was pretty early in the morning and there were no other customers, so Birdie was hovering around trying to urge some conversation out of him. She knew he appreciated the free breakfast, but his conversation consisted more of grunts. Birdie was used to his reticence, but she kept hoping. She knew Nott's background, his physical and mental injuries, and hoped her mothering attention would be good for him.

Nott didn't resent the familiarity but mostly wasn't interested. His was a solitary existence and he liked it that way. He didn't have to rely on anyone, and no one was relying on him. It was a bit lonely at times but suited him just fine.

The bells on the front door of the pharmacy jingled and in walked Paige.

"Well, good morning, Paige," said Birdie. "Roberta had to go off to visit her sister in the hospital, so she closed the Coffee House for the day." Birdie knew Paige's usual morning routine included coffee and conversation at the Cape Charles Coffee House. "Come on over here and sit up to the counter. My pastries might not be as fresh and flaky as Roberta's, but if you like I can put together a real breakfast for you like the one Nott's working on."

Nott looked up and saw Paige headed his way. Quickly he ducked his head back down and went back to work on his biscuits and gravy. Birdie topped up his cup of coffee. Nott had seen Paige around town, but never talked to her. He felt that she was way above his social status. She was beautiful and, he admitted to himself … she smelled great. Like a spring day in a flower garden.

Paige took a stool two down from Nott, giving him his space.

"You know, Miss Birdie, I haven't had a good calorie-filled down-home breakfast in an age. You go ahead on and load me up. I'll just not eat lunch to make up for it."

"Hmph. Some people appreciate my breakfasts," said Birdie nodding at Nott.

He looked up and gave her a weak smile. "Best meal of my day," he mumbled, and Birdie just glowed. She had finally gotten something out of him more than a grunt.

Paige looked over at him. Always the salesman she tried to engage him in conversation. "I've seen you walking down here of a morning. You eat all your meals here?"

"Breakfast," Nott muttered, shaking his head.

"Most important meal of the day," quipped Paige.

"Hmph," muttered Nott, taking another bite of biscuit dripping with sausage gravy.

"Nott's a wounded war hero," said Birdie. "Did you know that?"

Paige shifted one stool closer at the counter. This made Nott nervous and he tried to pull his head down further into his shoulders. He looked like a startled turtle.

"Were you in Iraq?" she asked.

"Mmmph," nodding.

"Oh, my. I don't think I've ever met a war hero before."

Nott scowled through his beard, his eyes flashing. "I ain't no hero," Nott stated forcefully. "Yeah, I was there. Yeah, I got blown up. But I ain't no hero, and I don't want to talk about it."

Both Birdie and Paige were taken aback by the strength and vehemence in Nott's statement. Paige saw the glance of disapproval from the ever-protective Birdie

"Oh, I'm so sorry," apologized Paige. "I didn't mean to pry."

"Mmmph." He returned to his breakfast while Paige and Birdie raised eyebrows at each other.

The bells on the front door jingled again, and in walked Senior Sheriff's Deputy Pablo Gerena and Cape Charles Police Department Sergeant Heath, laughing as though they had just shared a joke. Heath was an old-timer and had been a Sergeant on the CCPD for so long that nobody seemed to know his first name. He was always just Sergeant Heath.

"Paige!" exclaimed Pablo. He wandered over to the counter and took a stool right next to her with Heath on the other side of him.

"Having breakfast all alone?" he asked. He was used to her eating at the Cape Charles Coffee House with Donna or another of her buddies.

"I'm not alone," she stated forcefully. "I'm having breakfast with Nott."

At that Nott's head jerked up, then he quickly pulled back down trying to hide in his coat.

"Nott!" laughed the Deputy, turning to look at Heath, who laughed also. "Shoot, I didn't know he even knew how to speak." He leaned around Paige. "Hey, little man. Do you speak?" he prodded.

Nott quickly put down his fork, stood, nodded to Birdie and Paige, and walked out the door.

"See?" laughed Pablo. "He's a strange little nothing." Heath murmured his agreement.

Paige was furious. "Why you insensitive…" Paige said venomously. "It's no wonder people don't like cops. The two of you are like little boys throwing oyster shells at a cat. Mean, that's what you are."

"Hey, Paige-y," Pablo said, putting his hand on her arm.

Angrily she shrugged it off. "If you don't mind, I'll have my breakfast alone, without you two idiots making the milk curdle." She moved to the last stool at the counter and Birdie, throwing a disapproving glance at the two policemen, moved her coffee and silverware down to her. She leaned over to Paige, "Darn them! That's the first little inkling of talk I've gotten out of him, and they have to come in like high school bullies and spoil it."

Paige nodded. "I know Pablo thinks he owns me just because we've dated, but he doesn't! Besides, Nott and I were just … sort of talking."

Birdie shook her head. "Give a man a badge and a gun and he thinks he's God almighty himself. I think he's just compensating for some other … personal shortcoming."

Paige stifled a chuckle. "What can you tell me about Nott?" she asked.

Birdie shook her head. "Well, you know he's from a labor camp up to Machipongo. He got hurt really bad in the Army and now he's got that PS-whatever it is."

"Post-Traumatic Stress Disorder?" asked Paige.

"Yeah, that's it. Police Sergeant Heath told me about it. Of course, the way he put it was a lot crueler and cruder."

"Yeah. Those guys never got their heads out of high school. But didn't Deputy Pablo serve, too?"

PABLO WAS SOMEWHAT of a newcomer to Eastville, a "come here." He had been born in Norfolk and raised in Grandy Park public housing. As a kid, his friends were members of a violent gang of hoodlums who had emigrated from Costa Rica, but as much as they pushed him, he never got the full-body, face and neck tattoos or officially joined. He would have had to kill someone as part of his initiation, and he wanted to avoid that. This was a good thing because it meant that his police record was still clean when he finished high school. To escape the almost inevitable gang membership, Pablo enlisted in the Marines.

Pablo enjoyed his time in The Corps. It gave him an opportunity to exercise his brutal side without much worry of consequences. In fact, when he became a military policeman his ability to fight and inflict pain was somewhat of a benefit. Until that is, he learned the technique for subduing a subject called a "carotid resistance control hold," more commonly known as a choke hold. Using this technique Pablo was able to knock out the biggest, baddest, drunkest Marine in just seconds. It saved time, it saved pain, and his patrol partners would always egg him on to use it. The choke hold was banned by The Corps, though, and Pablo's overuse of it ended up in his being kicked out of the Marines with an Other Than Honorable (OTH) discharge.

He returned to Norfolk but found that with Hampton Roads being a military area, his OTH discharge made it hard to find a job beyond working on the docks. As a military policeman he had a certain amount of respect. As a dockworker, he had none, and it grated on him. He could still get into his occasional bar fight, which he enjoyed, but now there was the chance that he'd end up in jail, instead of getting a "blue brotherhood" pass.

To get a better job Pablo figured he needed to get away from the overwhelming Navy/Marine Corps presence in Norfolk, which easily could find out his discharge status, so he crossed the Chesapeake Bay Bridge-Tunnel to the Eastern Shore. He knew that there weren't a lot of jobs there, but he also knew that most young men looked to leave The Shore, not move to it. So, he applied for a position with the county sheriff's department and was quickly hired based on his military police experience. Pablo didn't mention his OTH discharge, and the Sheriff didn't bother to check very deeply into his background. He was just pleased to find someone with experience.

"**HOW COULD HE** be the Senior Deputy Sheriff if he got kicked out of the Marines?" asked Paige.

"Well, according to Heath what he did wasn't something he could be charged with, and he had experience as an MP, and the County was really hard up for deputies when he applied. I guess they just kind of 'winked' at it," said Birdie, her ponytail swaying as she slowly and ruefully shook her head.

Paige nodded, thinking that over. She had dated Pablo a couple of times. Maybe it was the "bad boy" attitude that excited her. He wasn't a keeper, for sure. But she'd had fun riding in his fast boat, and he usually had the money to take her to nice restaurants. But she had to admit there was a darker side to him that she didn't really know. She'd have to be careful.

Chapter Six

EACH MORNING AFTER his breakfast at Rayfield's, Nott returned to Cherrystone Creek and went to work to catch that day's meals. Starting with a little piece of bread left over from his breakfast he'd dangle it in the water until he was able to net a wandering blue crab. He'd cut up the crab and use the crab meat as bait until he was able to catch a few spot or perch. If they were of a size, he'd cut off a fillet or two for his own use. Usually, they were just too small and bony for that, so he kept them to bait his crab pots.

After he had a half-dozen of the little fish, he'd head off to work his line of crab pots. He had a short line of eight pots up the creek that he worked at least once a day. He'd shake the crabs out into an old bushel basket he had found on one of his deserted beach visits before rebaiting the pot with the fish he'd caught. Sometimes, when he was lucky, Nott would catch a fish in the pot too. Then he was "bait rich" and wouldn't have to skimp on the bait in any of the pots.

There were almost always crabs in his pots. Cherrystone, with its clean waters and abundant eelgrass, was a prime spawning area. Some days, if he was really lucky, he'd trap more than he could eat himself, and he'd take the overage and sell it to locals at the dock in Cape Charles. Pretty much, restaurants wanted the crab meat already picked.

This morning Nott got good catches in his first three pots. Of course, he threw the Sukes with eggs back in, as he did any undersized Jimmies. But it looked like he was going to have enough to sell some at the dock. He liked the extra money.

Nott headed for pot number four hoping for another good catch. He loved living on Cherrystone Creek. Except for the calls of the gulls and the ospreys, it was quiet. After his experience in the war, he craved the calm and quiet. He was fascinated constantly, watching the Great Blue Heron that frequented his creek, wading the shallows searching for fish or crabs. Nott kind of identified with the large bird. They both wanted to be left alone and to find their own food in the water without the interference of civilization.

He was always very watchful as he motored into the Creek. He knew of one mud slide where a pair of otters could sometimes be seen playing if he was quiet enough.

Today as he went further, the water getting shallower, he saw, something red in the water off up a side tributary. Ever the beachcomber looking for useful castoffs Nott shut down and pulled up his outboard and used his oar to pole his way up to the spot where he saw the color.

What he saw was in about two feet of water. He couldn't tell much of what it was. Some old fishnet wrapped around a package and weighted down with broken chunks of cement block. Dozens of crabs crawled around the item, squeezing in and out of the netting.

Nott had a plastic boat hook arrangement at the end of his oar, and leaned over snagging the net. It was heavy.

I guess those cinder blocks are holding it down, he thought. *Those and all the crabs. If I'm easy maybe I can get the crabs, too.*

Gently Nott brought the bundle towards the gunwale of the boat, still a good half-dozen crabs hanging on. Carefully and slowly he reached over the side and into the water, threading his fingers through the weave of the net. With painstaking care, he raised the package.

Darn thing's too heavy to just heave into the boat. Darn crabs are going to run when I fight with it.

Bracing his knees against the gunwale Nott set the boat hook down, reached into the water with his other hand and, with a great convulsive motion, fell back in the boat pulling the net-wrapped package with him. One of the pieces of cinder block hit him in the face and he muttered a curse.

Well, let's see what we've got. I suppose I can always use the section of fishnet. And the bigger chunks of block I'll just leave on the bottom under my house until I need them. Wish they had been drain tiles. I could have put them out for the peelers and got myself some soft shells. Oh, well. 'Wish in one hand and poop in the other ...'"

He started to unwrap the net, then dropped it, sitting back violently as though stung by a jelly fish. "Oh my God!" he exclaimed. There in a red-checked gingham dress and wrapped in the fishnet was a body.

Nott looked around frantically. Whether for help or for someone responsible for putting the body there he couldn't have said. *Oh, damn! Why'd this have to happen in my creek? Can I just slide the body back into the water and pretend I never found it?*

No. That might have been the best idea, but he just couldn't do it. *They'd find me. Once someone finds the body, they'll pin it on me. I guess I gotta do it.*

Arranging the body in the bottom of his boat, Nott turned back down Cherrystone. He slowly motored past the entrance to King's Creek and the Cape Charles Beach, rounding the jetty and turning into the harbor. Running in to the wharf Nott tied off his boat, climbed up on the wharf and hurried into the Harbor Master's office.

"A body!" Nott managed to gasp out.

"What is it you want, boy?" rasped the old Harbor Master. He was a crusty old retired waterman, too old to continue to work the water but too cantankerous to just sit and rock on the front porch.

Nott was intimidated. "I ... I found a..."

"Found a what?" the Harbor Master roared.

Nott took a step back.

"I ... I found a body."

"A body? Where?"

"Up Cherrystone Creek."

"Cherrystone? Is it still there?"

"N-n-no."

"Well, where the hell is it, then?"

Nott wasn't handling this well. "M-m-y boat."

"Well then, WHERE THE HELL IS YOUR BOAT?"

"Well, it's tied right here to your dock," said Nott.

"With the body still in it?"

Nott nodded.

"Oh, for Pete's sake. Show me. NOW!"

Nott led the man to his boat.

"Oh my gosh," the Harbor Master exclaimed when he saw the net entangled body in the bottom of the boat. "I thought you found someone who had drowned. That's no drowning victim. They've been ... murdered! That's a murdered body! Oh, my."

"That's what I've been trying to tell you," said Nott. The Harbor Master raced back to his office and picked up the phone.

"You wait right here," he ordered Nott. "Police? This is the Harbor Master. You need to send someone over here fast. I've got a dead body in a boat. No, at my office at the dock. No, I don't know who it is. No, I don't know how they died. YES, I'M SURE THEY'RE ALREADY DEAD. NOW GET SOMEONE OVER HERE."

Chapter Seven

WITH SIREN SCREAMING, Cape Charles Police Sergeant Heath came skidding up to the Harbor Master's office and tumbled out of his car with pistol in hand. A passing patrol boat from the Cape Charles Coast Guard Station saw the ruckus and, switching on their blue light, motored over also to see what was going on. All the noise and the flashing lights and the people started to get to Nott. His mind started playing tricks on him. He got confused and wasn't certain what was happening. The sirens had him looking for Humvee Front Line Ambulances. He didn't remember any gunfire or explosions, but he was losing touch with the reality of the moment. He tried to slip away, but Sergeant Heath prevented him from leaving. In fact, he suggested Nott take a seat in the back of his patrol car. Quietly and imperceptibly Nott began to retreat—not physically but into his mind. The flashing lights took him inexorably back to the battlefield. The loud yelling voices became the clamor of battle. The smell of death from the now stinking dead body became the aid station in the desert. His mind started reeling, and his legs started aching like his wounds were new. When Heath came over to confront him in the patrol car and begin questioning him as to where he had found the body, Nott became unresponsive. It wasn't that he refused to answer questions, he didn't even hear them. He was lost inside his head and couldn't escape the horror, but he couldn't straighten it out in his mind either.

To police Sergeant Heath Nott was simply another homeless bum who wouldn't cooperate.

"Where'd you find the body?" he demanded.

Nott simply sat there, hunched down into himself, staring vacantly into the front seat of the car.

Grabbing Nott's shoulder Heath shook him. "Was' a matter, boy? You deaf or sumpin?"

Nott just sat there, barely breathing.

"I think what happened was you saw that little girl, tried to get a little too friendly wit' her and when she fought you killed her. That how it happened, boy?"

Little girl? What little girl? Nott remembered a little boy standing by the side of the road when the IED blew his legs to pieces. *It was a little boy, not a little girl* he thought, then slumped deeper into his own mind.

Heath figured he had a real career-building arrest here. Roughly he pulled Nott from the back seat. Spinning him around he handcuffed his hands behind him and pushed him back into the car. Heath didn't mind Nott's head as he did so, and the back of it slammed into the frame of the car.

"Whoops. Sorry 'bout that, boy." Heath chuckled under his breath.

Pulling a small laminated card from his wallet Heath proceeded to read Nott his rights. "Do you understand these rights as I have 'splained them to ya?"

Nott just sat there.

"Well, I told ya. That's good enough for me." Lights flashing and siren blaring Sergeant Heath drove Nott to the Cape Charles Police Station, less than a quarter-mile away.

"What've you got?" asked the desk sergeant as Heath marched Nott into the station and pushed him down on a bench.

"First-degree murder," crowed Heath proudly. "I got him, and he ain't goin' nowhere. Killed him a little Mexican girl."

"Hmmm," said the desk sergeant. "Haven't had anything like that around here for a time. We keepin' him here or sending him up the road to the jail."

"I imagine we need to put him in county. They'll take care of him up there.

"Mexican girl," mused Heath. "Bet those beaners in county are going to love getting their hands on him." The desk sergeant nodded morosely.

They left Nott sitting handcuffed to the bench for hours. He didn't move. He didn't speak. He didn't look up. He was so quiet they almost had forgotten him when Chief Deputy Sheriff Gerena walked in with a haughty step. *Speaking of 'beaners'*, thought the desk sergeant sourly.

"This the murderer?" Gerena asked.

"Yep," was the reply.

"Well, give me some paperwork to sign and I'll take him off your hands. He okay?"

"Hasn't said a word."

"Read 'im his rights?"

"Of course."

"Okay. Well, hurry up the paperwork. I want to get shed of him before it gets too late to meet someone for dinner," Gerena smirked.

On the drive from Cape Charles to the Northampton County Jail in Eastville Gerena kept up a constant patter. "Them beaners in the jail gonna love you, boy. Killed one of their little girls? Be lucky if you don't get shivved before you even get processed."

Nott didn't respond. Nott didn't even hear him. He was lost in a murky world of his own.

Chapter Eight

THE BODY OF the unknown little girl was transported by ambulance from the dock in Cape Charles to Paige at Reese Funeral Home in Eastville. Because the Commonwealth of Virginia has a decentralized medical examiner system Paige had become the county's *ad interim* coroner. Because it was an *ad hoc* position it was unpaid, but Paige took it on as both her civic duty and as a salesman's way of showing the community how involved she was. To better perform her duties, she took classes in forensic medicine and criminal investigation.

Paige did not have the medical training to do a full-on autopsy, but there were various things about the dead girl that she could handle. She wasn't going to enjoy this. She'd worked with drowning victims before, and it wasn't pleasant. The longer they've been in the water the more advanced the decomposition and smell became, and with this one the crabs and fish had been feasting on the body, leaving ragged tears wherever the flesh was exposed. As usual the eyes were the first items to go, and Paige had difficulty with the empty sockets staring at her. She draped a small towel over the little girl's head so she could continue. She wasn't really spooked, just upset at the condition of the body of a little girl. But she soldiered on.

First, of course, she undressed and washed the body, noting that she was a pubescent Hispanic girl with no apparent wounds on her body—no stab marks or bullet holes or ligature marks. There were no identifying marks on the body, no scars or tattoos, and Paige was able to roll a set of fingerprints to send over to the sheriff's office. She doubted that it would do any good. In spite of what TV showed, fingerprints, especially of a little girl, seldom were of any use. But you never knew.

Continuing with her preliminary examination Paige determined that the girl had not been sexually violated. *Thank the good Lord, she thought. I don't think I could have handled that.* She shuddered.

Paige drew some tubes of blood for the Commonwealth's lab and set them aside. She didn't have the lab facilities to do toxicology screenings, but the lab in Norfolk would get them done in a hurry.

Paige did what little she could in her preliminary. Then covering the little girl with a sheet, and moving one of Billy's chilling six-packs, she slid the unidentified body into one of the refrigerated body units. Then Paige cleaned up from what she had done.

She had a lunch date with her friend Ann Webster Goffigon the Clerk of Court. They were going to meet at Machipongo Trading Company for a salmon salad panini, and she didn't want to be late, so washing up and making certain she didn't smell of "funeral home," she hurried to her car. After what she had just been through in her workroom she was not hungry, but she was anxious to talk with someone … living.

Ann Webster was already seated at one of the small tables drinking an iced cafe con leche. The Trading Company was one of the few places that had Wi-Fi, and Ann was online and fiddling with the Internet on her cell phone. Looking up she said, "Hey, girl," as Paige joined her.

"You been here long?" asked Paige.

"Naw."

Paige waited patiently for Ann Webster to finish online and put her phone away. "So, what's happening over at the courts?"

"Well," Ann said conspiratorially, "you heard about the murder down in Cape Charles?"

"Yeah," responded Paige. "I just finished my preliminary on the body."

Ann sat upright with a surprised look. "Oh! And what did you find? Anything interesting? How did she die? Do you know who she was?"

"Now Ann Webster, you know I can't talk about it. It's an open case. The sheriff would have a hissy fit, and I could kiss any more county work goodbye."

"Well, sure, but ... well, is there anything ... strange about it? About her?"

"What are you digging for?" Paige replied. "Honestly, I didn't find anything except the poor girl is dead."

"Well," said Ann, "I just wondered ... since that strange little man, James Nottingham Smith was involved ... you know. Did he ... *do* anything to her?"

Paige was knocked back in her seat. "What? Who said anything about Nott being involved?"

"*Nott?* Do you know him?"

"No, I don't really know him," said Paige. "I just met him at Rayfield's one morning and tried to talk with him. I think Birdie was trying to hook us up. Who said he's involved with this?"

"Well, they brought him into the jail a few hours ago. He was all shackled up. They said they had him on suspicion of murder."

"*They what!?* Who arrested him?"

"Why, Deputy Gerena, of course. Sergeant Heath called him from the Cape Charles PD, and he hustled on down there to take him into custody. He's sitting over in the jail up here right now!"

Paige stood up so quickly her chair fell over backward. "Those idiots! Did they get a doctor to look at him?"

"I don't know," said Ann very quietly.

Paige could see how unnerved her friend had become from her outburst but couldn't deal with that now. Dropping a ten-dollar bill on the café table she rushed out the door.

Chapter Nine

PAIGE BURST THROUGH the door at the Northampton County Sheriff's office, with fury in her eyes.

"Where's Deputy Gerena?"

Junior, the on-duty desk sergeant, leaned back in his chair and mildly looked up at her, adding to her fury. "Why, hi, Miss Paige. What can I do for you?" He was a middle-aged man, balding with a bad comb-over and an overhanging belly that hid his belt buckle and much of his lap. He'd been a fixture at the Sheriff's Department since Paige was a baby.

"Junior, you can get that egg-sucking Gerena out here. Now!"

Junior hiked up in his desk chair, trying to look officious, pushed a button on the telephone. "Can you come up front, please? We have a ... situation."

A moment later Pablo Gerena sauntered out from the back of the station.

"Paige," he enthused. "What's up?"

"Did you check the missing person reports to see if you could find our dead girl?"

"Well, sure. Both here and up in Accomack, and I sent an inquiry across to Virginia Beach and Norfolk."

"How about her fingerprints? Did you run them through AFIS?"

"Well, honey – "

"Don't call me 'honey'," Paige snapped.

"Whew! Ok. As you know a kid that young is almost certainly not going to have prints on file."

"So, you didn't check them?" she snapped accusatorily.

"Wait a minute! What are you getting on my case for? You got PMS or something?"

Paige went ballistic. Her eyes bulged and her face turned red. "What?"

Pablo quickly moved out of reach behind the counter.

"I'll file a complaint on you with the sheriff," she yelled. "With the county commission. How dare you…"

Pablo raised his hand defensively. "Look, Paige, I'm sorry. I'm just not used to being interrogated by a g—, a civilian."

"Well, have you done anything?"

"Sure, but we haven't found anything out. She's just a nobody. A Juanita Doe." Gerena smiled as though he had made a clever joke.

Paige raised her eyebrows until they almost disappeared in her hairline. "A…"

"Heck. Anyway Paige. Why are you so concerned? It's just another migrant worker. It's not like she was anyone."

"Like she..." Paige stammered. Changing directions, she demanded, "And I understand you've made an arrest in her murder?"

"Sure have," Gerena said proudly. "Got that little retard weirdo that lives out in the oyster house. Caught him red-handed with the body. Got him dead to rights."

"'Red-handed with the body'?" she asked. "I heard that he brought the body to the Harbor Master's office, that he found it while he was working his line of crab pots."

"Well, that's the excuse he gave. I figure he raped her then killed her then dumped the body where the crabs would dispose of it."

Paige was beside herself. "If that's your brilliant theory, then why did he later retrieve the body and bring it into town?"

"Well, he probably—"

"And she was not sexually assaulted."

"How do you know that?"

"I'm the coroner, remember? I performed the 'post' on the body."

"Oh. Yeah. Right."

"So, what you've got is a good Samaritan finding a body and instead of just pretending he never saw it, or just reporting where it was so that you'd have to get your fat ass out there to retrieve it, he brings it in ... and gets arrested for his trouble? Is that pretty much it?"

Pablo had never seen Paige so furious. "Well, yeah, I guess."

"Where is he?" she demanded. "You take me to him right now."

"Well, Paige, he's kind 0f ... not doing real well right now."

"What do you mean by that?" she demanded. "Did you beat him up in his cell?"

"No, no, nothing like that. It's just that he ... well, he's kind of not responding."

"What?"

"Oh, he's okay and all. He's awake and breathing and everything. He's just kind of out of it. Like maybe he's on drugs." He took her out back to one of the jail cells.

In the cell, Nott was curled up in a tight ball in the corner. His eyes were open, but unseeing. His breathing was regular but shallow.

"Did you call a doctor for him?" she demanded.

"What for? He's fine, just faking it. There aren't any signs of trauma or anything, and he's awake and breathing."

"Well, the little girl he found and brought in had no signs of injury either. EXCEPT FOR THE FACT THAT SHE WAS DEAD.

"This man is a war hero. He got blown up by an IED in Iraq. And has PTSD. You were supposedly in the Marines. You should understand that. Look at him. He's almost unconscious. He doesn't even know we're here." Paige stamped her foot furiously.

"I want him released right now. Into my custody."

Pablo shook his head. "Well, Paige, I don't know that I can do that. He's in here for murder."

"Has he been before a judge?"

"Well, no, not really. He's kind of not in a condition to go before the judge, you know."

"So, he hasn't been arraigned?

"Do you have any sort of evidence other than your flaming imagination?"

"Now wait a minute," protested Pablo. "Y'ain't got no call to talk to me like that."

"Is there any evidence?" asked Paige patiently.

"Well, no, not as such," he replied.

"Then help me get him up and out to my car. I'll sign a custody receipt for him."

"Now, Paige, he ain't got nothin' keepin' him here on The Shore. He's what we call a 'flight risk.' Besides, what do you want him for? You got somethin' goin' on with him?"

Deputy Gerena had gone too far. Paige rounded on him, her face pale with almost manic rage. "You … will … release … this … man … now … and assist me in getting him to my car. Do you understand?"

"Uh, yes ma'am," he managed to say. He went into the cell and, standing over Nott, nudged him with his toe. "Let's go, boy."

Paige had to restrain herself from snatching the black-leather slapjack from his side pocket and hitting him with it. "Help him up!" she ordered.

"But he smells horrible."

"You get one side and I'll get the other. Come on, we'll walk him to my car."

It was almost like maneuvering a drunk. Nott didn't seem to be aware of where he was going or hear their directions, but at least he did maintain his sense of balance, so they didn't have to actually carry him.

They slid him into the passenger seat and Paige reached in to fasten his seatbelt.

"Okay," said Pablo. "Now what? Where are you going to take him?"

"There's an apartment upstairs at the funeral home. I'm going to put him in there."

"You're not staying there, are you?" Pablo asked.

"No, I'll stay in my apartment out at the beach. I'll leave him my cell number so he can call if he needs anything."

Pablo looked at her dubiously. "You be careful. You don't really know what kind of a nut this guy is."

"I'll be fine. I'm going to call Ann Webster to come help me get him settled. If you need him for anything, just call me."

She drove off, screeching her tires and showering Pablo with gravel as she went.

Chapter Ten

FOR MOST OF a week Nott had been staying pretty much to himself in the upstairs apartment. Paige would go up and try to talk with him, but he pretty much just sat on the bed watching television. Paige finally shamed him into bathing, shaving and brushing his hair, by telling him that she didn't want her sheets ruined. While he was in the shower, she took his clothes away to wash.

She gave him a bathrobe that had been her daddy's to bundle up in while she washed his clothes. It was fortunate she got his clothes away from him. It took three trips through the washer to get them smelling clean. Nott kept complaining about not having his own clothes, but Paige told him he'd just have to be patient. He actually wasn't too bad looking when he was cleaned up.

"You're going to the church supper with me this weekend," Paige told him.

"Ain't," he replied.

"Listen, the only reason you're not still sitting in a cell like a vegetable is that I vouched for you. They released you in my custody. That means that if I'm going to the church supper, so are you."

"Like this?" he asked.

"Tell you what," said Paige. "I'll cut your hair and get you some of my brother's clothes to wear."

"You a barber, too?"

"Well ... sort of. You know I have to prepare bodies for their viewings, so I know a little bit about cutting and styling hair."

"You're gonna use the same stuff on me that you use on dead people?" he asked, seeming perturbed.

"Oh, for Pete's sake," she said. "Get over yourself. I always wash and disinfect them between uses, and it's not like you can catch 'dead' from them."

"Well ... y'ain't givin' me no clothes from a dead man to wear?"

"Check and see if they have pockets. No pockets in corpse clothes, you know. No, I'll get you some of my brother Billy's clothes. Last I saw him he wasn't dead. Wasn't much good for anything, but he was alive and drinking. Beer."

"Man, I could use some of that myself."

"I do not have any drinking alcohol on the premises. You'll just have to do without. If you behave, maybe I'll buy you a six-pack later on."

"Like being married," he muttered under his breath.

"WHAT?"

"Nuthin'."

"All right then."

The supper at Paige's church, Foxtown United Methodist, was that Saturday afternoon. Apart from it being good business for her to be seen there, Paige really wanted to go. She wasn't what anyone would call "a foodie," but she loved the food of the Eastern Shore. She almost called it *cuisine* as she was thinking about it, but that would be just too uppity. This would be just good old 'down home' food.

Nott cleaned up pretty well, and although he didn't want to go with her, Paige didn't give him a choice. She had brought him some clean dungarees and a white oxford cloth shirt from Billy's, and even bought him a pair of sneakers at Rose's in Exmore. Cleaned up and dressed up you'd hardly recognize him.

Actually, his anonymity was a good thing. The ladies of the church were fascinated by this quiet stranger and went out of their way to cater to him. They didn't realize that this was the same "murderer" that Paige had taken in. "You've got to try some of these fritters," one would say. "I made them. Do you like them?"

Another would approach him and ask, "You from around here? Or you just visiting? You relative to someone in the church?"

It was like water drip drip dripping on a rock. All of the motherly attention incessantly but lovingly applied, began to wear him down. Although Nott didn't go into much detail, he did allow that he was from Machipongo, a while back. When he told that he had been badly injured in Iraq it set the ladies off even more, each one trying to outdo the other in being nice to him. Some even brought daughters and nieces over to meet him, which kind of made him quiet again. He wasn't growing gregarious, but Nott was beginning to come out of his shell.

The supper was a fund raiser for the church and open to everyone. It was set up in the church yard in the shade of the trees on folding tables and chairs. It had been mentioned in the EASTERN SHORE NEWS, and the turnout was pretty good. And the food! The food was wonderful. Clam fritters, crab imperial, fried chicken, roast oysters, and all sorts of salads and side dishes, like corn-on-the-cob and stewed okra. There was enough sweet tea to float a skipjack. Tomatoes were in abundance, and for desert there were sweet potato pie, peach cobbler, apple pie, watermelon, and homemade ice cream for the kids. Paige ate delicately, keeping up appearances, but Nott ate like it was his first and last meal. Fortunately, the ladies of the church had been prepared for large numbers and large appetites, and they kept up with him, enjoying his enjoyment.

After a while, Pablo showed up in his brown sheriff's uniform. Paige was off to the side chatting with some folks while Nott was still eating at the table. Pablo got a plate of food, and sat down nodding pleasantly to Nott, whom he did not even recognize. Nott kind of froze up in the presence of the deputy, and as soon as he had finished his food he got up and moved quickly to Paige's side and protection.

Pablo glanced up, and seeing Nott in context with Paige, glowered. He walked over to them.

"Paige, what the hell are you thinking bringing him here?" he demanded.

Nott immediately shut down and retreated back into his shell.

"Watch your language, Pablo; you're in a churchyard."

"Yeah, well just the same, are you crazy bringing him here amongst these church folks?"

"Would you rather I locked him in the root cellar or one of the body coolers?" responded Paige.

"C'mon, Paige. You know what I mean. He's suspected of murder."

"Maybe by you, Pablo. But you haven't any proof. There's no evidence. None except your hate for him."

"I don't hate him," said the deputy. "I just don't trust him. He's sneaky. And he's an unemployed bum, squatting in that oyster house in the middle of Cherrystone Creek. Why do you think he does that? What do you imagine he does in there?"

"I guess he just tries hard to live by himself, quietly. With no hassles or harassment from people like you and Heath," she responded. "Why don't you just leave him alone?"

During all this Nott just stood silently by, his head down, hands stuffed into his pockets.

"Come on, Nott," said Paige. "Suddenly it's not as much fun here anymore."

"Ah, Paige," said Pablo, trying to mollify her. "Come on. I'm just doing my job."

"No," declared Paige. "Your job would be investigating this unknown little girl's murder and trying to find some evidence. Trying to find out why and who and where. Instead, you are just taking the easiest way, trying to hang it on poor Nott, who just happened to be at the wrong place at the wrong time. That's not doing your job."

She grabbed Nott by the elbow and pulled him to her car. Getting in, they drove off.

Sergeant Heath, the man who originally arrested Nott, was at the dinner, also. He wandered over to Pablo. Nodding at the car he said, "Kind of beating your time with Paige, ain't he?"

Pablo just ground his teeth.

Chapter Eleven

PAIGE STILL HAD her day-to-day job to attend to. Luckily a major part of that job was sales, and an important part of the sales was schmoozing. The more people she knew, the more business she would get.

That night was a meeting of the board of the Citizens for a Better Eastern Shore. Years ago, Paige would have been in favor of as much development as The Shore could take. The more urbanized the better. Now, with age came an appreciation for the beauty and simplicity around her. Paige was so happy when asked to be a member of the board.

But tonight's meeting was not on the health of The Shore. Instead everyone, except Paige, wanted to talk about the murder. She wished she hadn't attended.

"Hey, Paige. Did you ever find out who that unknown little girl is?" asked Nora peering over her horn-rimmed reading glasses.

"No, Nora, we still haven't been able to identify her."

"Did you take her fingerprints?" asked someone else.

Paige sighed. Everyone had watched too much CSI on television. "Yes, of course we did, but unless someone has been arrested or in the military their fingerprints probably aren't on record. We're talking about a girl who's only about fourteen."

"Oh, yeah. Of course," the questioner said. "Well, how about facial recognition?"

Frustrated Paige blew a stray hair out of her face. "Oh, come on! We don't have that kind of software on The Shore."

"Well ... how about missing person reports?" asked Jim, leaning into Paige's personal space.

"Jim, don't you think that the sheriff would check those?" Paige was getting annoyed. "They tell me they checked here and Accomack and even the western shore. No, there is no report." She turned to the director.

"Donna, shouldn't we be discussing business?"

"Yes, we should," replied Donna. "We've got a number of subjects on our agenda."

"Yes, but Paige," chimed in a silver-haired old-timer named Ches, "what are you going to do?"

"What am I going to do? I'm just the unofficial coroner, Ches. I'm going to have to ask the state medical examiner in Norfolk for help. Maybe they'll be able to come up with something. I'm not the medical examiner, you know. I don't have all the fancy gear they do." Paige peered around the conference table, a look of frustration on her face.

"Come on, now. We've got business to discuss, don't we?"

The meeting finally got back on track, but people kept looking over at Paige as if they just *had* to ask her more questions about the body. As soon as the final gavel fell Paige was out the door and into her car before she could get buttonholed for more questions. *Man, what a pain,* she thought. *All because of a free part-time job. That'll teach me to volunteer.*

Paige drove by the funeral home to check on Nott before going home to her apartment out at the beach. Nott was wrapped in his blanket, snoring softly. Open on the floor next to him was a tattered copy of AN EASTERN SHORE SKETCHBOOK that he had been reading before he went to sleep. Paige left the light on in the hall just in case he woke in the middle of the night wondering where he was.

Back in her own apartment, with the breeze blowing in off The Bay, Paige lay on her bed. *What on earth am I doing?* she wondered. *I'm just a small-town undertaker and now I have an unidentified body in my 'fridge, and a stranger living in my upstairs apartment ... a broken stranger, both physically and mentally. Damn, I'm not a cop. And I'm not a shrink. I'm not even a social worker. What the heck am I getting myself into? And it's not like I'm even attracted to him. At least that would be an excuse. Maybe not a good one, but an excuse.*

The next morning, not really feeling domestic but feeling obligated, Paige drove to the funeral home and cooked breakfast for Nott. As they sat eating, Paige tried to draw him out about his past. She tried it in a chatty way. She didn't want him to think she was interrogating him.

"So, you grew up around here?"

"Mmmph."

"Someone said you were from Machipongo."

"Mmmph."

"Yeah, I've lived here all my life. Did you go to Northampton High School?"

"Uh, uh. Didn't go to school."

"Oh. Home-schooled."

"No schooled."

"So, do you still have people around?"

"Nope."

"Oh." Paige took another bite of grits and a sip of coffee. "Want some more coffee?"

He held out his mug.

"D'ja ever go to any of the football games at the high school?"

"Naw. Couldn't. Pappy wouldn't 'low it. Said he didn't want me mixin' with any of those townies."

"Like me," said Paige. Then she quickly realized her mistake.

"Oh, I..." Nott began to turn red. "I didn't mean nuthin' like..." He began to shut down and draw into himself again.

"I'm so sorry," said Paige. "That was a smart-ass thing for me to say. I sometimes let my mouth overrun my brain. I'm sorry. I really didn't mean that the way it sounded."

But Nott had withdrawn. Not near as bad as when he was in the jail, but he hung his head down, wouldn't look at her and wouldn't say anything.

"Nott, I'm really sorry," Paige said again. "Look, I have to do some work. You can stick around here while I'm working, or you can go back upstairs. Whatever you want."

Nott rose. "Thanks," he said, motioning at the breakfast dishes. Then he slowly climbed the stairs back to his apartment.

Paige smacked herself on the forehead. *I almost had him talking again,* she thought to herself. *And then I had to let my big mouth spoil it.*

Paige worked in her office until lunchtime. She was going to go with Pam Kellam, the postmistress, for fried trout and hush puppies at Yuk Yuk & Joe's. The post office was just down the street, so Paige picked Pam up on her way past.

Pam was carrying on about the quirks of some of the customers she had seen that morning as they drove to the restaurant. They grabbed a booth when they went in and gave their orders to the waitress.

"I also want a cheeseburger and French fries to go," said Paige.

"You really hungry?" asked Pam.

"No, I still have Nott living up in the apartment at the home. I want to take him something, or else he won't eat anything."

"Nott!" exclaimed Pam. "That drifter's still living with you?"

"He's not living with me," protested Paige. "I'm just letting him stay up in the apartment 'til this whole mess is cleared up."

"Mmm hmph. What does Deputy Sexy think about you living with another man?"

"Oh, come on, Pam," said Paige. "I'm not living with him. I'm not even living in the house. It's like he's a renter. And besides, Pablo doesn't own me. We just date some."

"Right. Well, you know what the talk is?"

"What talk?"

"People are saying that you're harboring a murderer."

"What? Who's saying that?"

"Well, Paige, you know I can't tell you that. Like you can't tell me about what you found when you looked at the body of the little girl."

"Well..."

"And they tell me that Deputy Pablo is upset with your relationship with Nott."

"THERE'S NO RELATIONSHIP! WITH EITHER OF THEM!"

Chapter Twelve

PAIGE DROPPED THE cheeseburger off with Nott then drove over to the sheriff's department to confront Pablo. She walked in quietly but with the icy glare of a pit-viper ready to strike.

"So, I hear you're upset with me putting Nott up in the apartment," she stated.

"No, no, not really. I…"

"The word around town is that you think I'm harboring a murderer and that the only reason he isn't in jail is that I'm dating you. Of course, that's kind of screwed up. If I'm dating you why would I be protecting him in my apartment?"

Pablo sat kicked back in his desk chair, his black engineer boots on the desktop and a toothpick in the side of his mouth. "That's a good question, Paige. You are dating me, and you are taking care of him. Don't you think that's kind of … well, strange? Or at least in poor taste?" questioned Pablo. "After all, you are my girl." He gave her a smarmy grin.

That set Paige off. "Your girl? Who says I'm 'your girl?' Since when do you 'own' me to say I'm 'your girl?' Since when do you have any say over what I do? Or what I think? Or where I go? Your girl?"

Pablo stood and quickly looked around. "Not so loud, Paige."

"Not so loud? Are you afraid someone will question your manhood? If they think you can't control 'your girl'?"

"C'mon, Paige. Can't we be nice to each other?"

Paige let her anger recede. *Why am I so angry with him? He's just trying to make me like him. Maybe that's it. I don't want someone else thinking for me.*

"Okay, let's talk about this case," said Paige.

"I wasn't able to determine any cause of death. Have you contacted the Commonwealth Medical Examiner?"

"Not yet," replied Pablo. "I mean, it's only a migrant worker. No one is looking for her. It's an undetermined mishap."

Paige's anger fired back up. "Undetermined mishap? What on earth are you talking about? This was a murder."

"Well, yeah. But if we don't know who the victim is, no one has filed a missing person, we don't have any suspects, and no one really cares. We're going to leave it as an open case but call it an undetermined mishap."

"The hell, you say!" Paige seldom swore, but this was pushing her over her limits. "I'm not going to just forget about it."

"Paige, you don't have any real legal standing here, you know."

"What do you mean? I'm the coroner."

"No, not really. You're not sworn, and you don't have a badge. You just help out with the occasional dead body. But you're not really the coroner. You're not really anything but a civilian volunteer."

The smoke was almost ready to pour from Paige's ears.

"Fine," she snarled.

"C'mon, Paige," Pablo pleaded, trying to placate her. "Don't fight with me. I'm just doing my job. Give me a break huh?"

Paige just glared.

"You know what? I'll bet it was those four boys from the high school yellow jackets football team did it," said Pablo.

"What four boys?"

"There are these four football players who hang together and have gotten in trouble over girls before. I've had to answer a couple of calls to the high school because of them gettin' a little too familiar with some of the girls. Trouble is their fathers are all big shots, so the sheriff won't let me do nothin'. Gettin' away with stuff ... well, that just makes them more of a problem."

"What have they done?" Paige asked.

"Well, with the white girls they've just kind of ... well, put their hands where they shouldn't. But they usually stop as soon as the girl complains."

"And the non-whites?"

Pablo kind of chewed his lip when he answered. "Well, you know we don't have a lot of control over what happens to the black or Mexican girls."

"What's happened?"

"Well, they sometimes get a little rambunctious with them."

"Rambunctious?" Paige pressed.

"Aw, Paige. Yeah, they might back one of those girls into the corner and feel her up some."

"And that's all right with you?" she fumed.

"No. Of course not. But—"

"But what?"

"Well, like I said, their fathers are pretty powerful in the county. And it's the school that complains. The girls and their families never say nothin', so ain't nothin' I can do."

"There 'ain't nothin' you can do,' or there's nothing you're willing to do?"

"Ah, shit, Paige…" She looked up sharply. "I mean shoot, Paige. It'd be worth my badge if I got too pushy on them boys."

"So, you just let them think they can get away with their actions," she stated angrily.

"Probably wasn't them no how," Pablo said.

"Who are they?" Paige demanded.

"What?"

"Who are they? I might want to talk with them."

"Paige, I told you, you're not part of this anymore."

"I can find out from the school if I have to. Now, who are they?"

Pablo seems cowed by her anger, and Pablo gives in. "There's Bubba Wilkins, Billy Ray Point, John Marion Heath, and Chris Williams. But, Paige, don't go messing around with them. Their daddies are very influential. Just take my advice and accept that this is just a mysterious death of an unknown victim due to mishap."

Paige leaned in and gave him a kiss on the cheek. "Thanks for the information."

Pablo smiled broadly at the kiss. "Now don't go spreading that to your friends like Pam or Ann," Pablo warned.

"Me?" protested Paige, and with a satisfied smile, she went out the door.

Chapter Thirteen

IT WAS A beautiful Eastern Shore evening. Temperatures were moderate, there was a slight breeze blowing and the sky had only a few puffy white clouds.

Pam called Paige. "Hey, girl. How about going out and sitting on the sandbar with me while we watch the sunset?"

"Fantastic," Paige enthused. "I'd love it. What can I bring?"

"Just your own sweet self ... unless you happen to have a nice bottle of wine. I'll supply the towels and the beach chairs and a cooler full of ice."

"I'll see you in fifteen minutes," said Paige.

Paige had a bottle of steel-fermented Church Creek Chardonnay from Chatham Vineyards in Machipongo. It had been in her refrigerator for a while as she saved it for a special occasion. *This is that occasion*, she decided. She put the wine, two glasses, a corkscrew, and some fine Brie in a small cooler and met Pam at the dock on The Gulf, the shallow creek that led out into The Bay.

Pam had already loaded her center console Boston Whaler with aluminum beach chairs, towels, and her own cooler. The tide was pretty low, so they slowly threaded their way out the channel to the sandbar which sat exposed, deserted but for a couple of seagulls. The sun was already getting low in the sky.

"This is heaven," said Paige, digging her toes into the wet sand.

"One of my favorite places and favorite times of the day," replied Pam.

"So, what's going on with the murder?"

Paige had intended to ply Pam with the wine to get her talking about the possibilities in the murder, but it didn't look as though there would be any hesitation on Pam's part. She was ready to swap any and all gossip. Well, "local intelligence," as she called it.

"I really don't have anything, Pam. She's still a Jane Doe."

"Well, have you figured out how she died?"

"No. There's no sign of wounds. She doesn't have ligature marks around her neck."

"What kind of marks?"

"Ligature. You know, like if she'd been strangled by a light cord or something." Pam frowned her understanding. "She hasn't got any apparent bruising, and there's no sign of sexual abuse. It's really a mystery.

"But how 'bout you?" asked Paige, swirling the wine in her glass. "You know pretty much everything that's going on. You hear anything at the post office?"

"No," lamented Pam. "Everyone keeps asking me instead of telling me. No one seems to have any idea of what happened.

"Oh, there's some guessing." Pam took a sip of her wine. "Some people think that she's a Mexican migrant worker whose boss tried to get her to pick a little more than tomatoes, and when she wouldn't he killed her. Others think maybe someone just passing through picked her up on the highway. Nobody knows."

The post mistress continued, "she's still little, so some people think that it might have been another migrant worker from her camp who wanted her and maybe when she wouldn't give out, he punched her so hard in the stomach that it broke something inside and killed her."

"All decent guesses," said Paige, "but I don't see any actual evidence in any of them."

Pam frowned. "I love mysteries," she said, "but this one doesn't seem to have any clues."

Paige nodded. They sat watching the red sun lowering toward the horizon. It was so clear they could just make out the bluffs on the other side of The Bay.

Then they heard a mechanical roaring sound from the south. It was headed their way. Paige knew what it was and shook her head.

"Darn it. Here comes Pablo in his Cigarette boat. I wanted to just sit here and enjoy the sunset and the friendship."

"You don't have to go with him," Pam said.

"Yes ... yes, I do," said Paige. "He'll expect it, and he's still a little tender about the going over I gave him about this murder.

He wants to close it out as unsolvable, 'death by unknown mishap.' I think he's being lazy."

"Sounds like he doesn't want to solve it."

"Mmm," said Paige. "Here he comes."

Looking south they could follow the screaming sound to a fast-moving sliver of yellow followed by a huge rooster tail.

"Likes to make an entrance, doesn't he?" snorted Pam. "Compensating, I guess. How do you stand riding in that thing?"

Paige smirked. "When you get going fast enough you leave a lot of the sound behind. And, Pam, I have to confess I really get off on the speed of that thing."

"Get off?"

"NO! You know what I mean. I really enjoy going so fast when the water's smooth. Even when there's a light chop, we just skim across it. Of course, when it's rough all bets are off. That thing will kill your kidneys."

As he drew close to the sandbar on the bayside, Pablo idled down. "Paige," he called, "c'mon. Let's go for a sunset ride. Then I'll take you to dinner at Mallard Cove."

"I'm here with Pam," she complained.

"Ah, Pam won't mind, will you Pam?"

Pam looked daggers at him, but said to Paige, "Go ahead. Our date is almost over. I wasn't going to feed you. He will."

Paige called to Pablo, "Okay, hang on. Let me get my things together."

Pablo nosed his boat into the shallow water and waited for her. The boat only drew 27" of water, so Paige was able to wade out to it without getting too wet. Pablo grabbed her hands and pulled her aboard.

"Thanks, Pam," she called as Pablo backed off the sandbar. Pam waved a hand. Paige thought it should have been a finger.

Pointing the bow back south Pablo said, "Better get ready." He slammed the throttles forward. Paige hadn't been ready, and she was thrown violently into the thick padding of the copilot seat in the boat's cockpit. Pablo looked over at her trying to get straightened out and laughed. Paige didn't think it was that funny, but the noise from the twin Mercury 565 racing engines and the howl of the wind kept her from making a biting comment.

It was a calm flat evening on the water, and the boat was soon topping sixty knots heading south toward Cape Charles and the Chesapeake Bay Bridge-Tunnel beyond.

As they approached Fisherman Island, Pablo eased back on the throttles. He wasn't as much concerned about the island being a federal wildlife refuge as he was about the narrow, twisty channel leading to the Mallard Cove Marina where he moored his boat. Running hard aground on a bed of oyster shells was pretty much guaranteed to remove lots of paint and fiberglass from the bottom of your boat.

Proceeding at a high idle Pablo entered the marina and skillfully backed his boat into his slip. One of the dock boys was there to help him with his lines, and as he moored, he waved to some friends standing there lusting after his boat.

He jumped ashore and helped Paige climb out. He thanked the dock boy, but stiffed him for a tip, as he walked Paige to the Cove Beach Bar. Paige noticed the slight and gave the dock boy an embarrassed grimace. The boy shrugged his shoulders as though it were a regular thing.

Mallard Cove Marina, located at the very tip of the Eastern Shore, was fairly new, and very nice. The developers had totally refurbished the old restaurant and included the Cove Beach Bar at the front. The food was exquisite, and the atmosphere was all about boating. The wall that had stood between the old patio and the restaurant was gone, and in its place was what looked like an ultra-wide sportfish's transom and cockpit, complete with exhaust pipes, a waterline, and faux bottom paint. In gold leaf with green outline were the words "Irish Luck" and the hailing port underneath read "Mallard Cove, VA." Extra deep teak covering boards with polyester resin on top served as the bar surface, with seats on the parking lot side, so they all faced toward the water. The other side had an open service area with a low knee wall, providing the view of charter boat row.

Pablo loved the macho fisherman feel. Paige loved the water view and watching the regular denizens of charter boat row. Sometimes some of their customers were too much to take, however. Like tonight.

One of the charter boats had come back in after a long day in the hot sun with a fish box limited out. The boisterous fishermen, down from Long Island, were pretty much limited out too—on beer. A hot day on the water and an over-generous supply of suds can create problems.

One red-faced gentleman decided that Paige would be happier sitting at his table than "with that spic," Pablo. Paige decided that the best way to handle the situation was to just ignore him.

Unfortunately, beer and bravado don't like to be ignored, and the fisherman arose, albeit unsteadily, and walked to Paige and Pablo's table. Turning his back to Pablo he drunkenly leaned over Paige. "Come on, sweetheart. Leave this loser and come have a drink with me. I got more money than he's got teeth, and no one pretty to spend it on."

Pablo jumped to his feet and, wrapping his right arm around the drunk's throat so that his Adam's apple was in the crook of his elbow, pulled him up away from Paige. Behind the man's head, Pablo grabbed his right wrist with his left hand and applied pressure.

"Stop it," screamed Paige. "You're killing him."

Pablo smiled at her. "No, it's just a little something they taught me in the Corps." He held on for only about ten seconds and the man slipped unconscious to the floor.

"It's called a Carotid Resistance Control Hold. You just cut off the blood flow to his brain for a couple of seconds, and boom. He's unconscious. 'Course he's gonna have one heck of a headache when he wakes up. Hmph, on top of his hangover, he's not going to be worth much for a while."

The man's friends had jumped from their seats when he slumped unconscious but withered under Pablo's fierce glare. Pablo picked the man up off the floor and put him back in his chair with his head on his arms on the table as though he were asleep. "Nighty night, pretty boy."

Chapter Fourteen

NORTHAMPTON COUNTY SHERIFF'S Department Senior Deputy Pablo Gerena was raised in the Grandy Village public housing complex of Norfolk, VA. It was a gritty existence. His father was gone, and his Salvadoran mother worked nights as a cleaner in a restaurant for minimum wage. She'd put him to bed, kiss him good night, and she would be gone until the next morning. As a teenager, he was expected to be able to take care of himself during the night.

Of course, once he was a teenager, he'd wait for his mother to go, climb out of bed, and go hang out with his friends. Because of his Salvadoran heritage, his friends tended always to be tattooed gang members.

Pablo idolized his tough gang "brothers," and they tolerated him. But he was only a hanger-on, and they wanted him as a full-fledged member. They were all covered in tattoos, some with the gang name, others with tribal symbols. Many of the members even proudly sported faces completely obscured by tattoos. They kept pushing Pablo to visit their tattoo parlor and begin his transformation process, but he was afraid of the needle. He was afraid of his *mami* as well. He did get a 7 tattooed on his left calf and a 6 on his right calf in small letters. They added up to "13," symbolizing his dedication to the gang. And he had his own machete, which he kept well-honed and oiled. But he left the machete with a friend when he had to go home, and he kept his tattoos hidden by long pants and, most importantly, he did not participate in the brutal killings the gang enjoyed. When someone had "disrespected" a member of his group, the gang took their machetes and baseball bats to exact retribution. They eschewed the use of guns preferring more medieval modes like knives and clubs where the kill is more personal and can be made more excruciating. When Pablo saw them getting ready for one of these brutal raids, he always managed to be somewhere else.

But Pablo did participate in other of the gang's activities. He liked the powerful feel of extortion and was happy to throw his weight around scaring the civilians. And he enjoyed the gang's prostitution business. He was always willing to force-feed alcohol or drugs to the victims to keep them subdued. Pablo was tall and had Latin good looks and was so good at finding young runaways and talking them into partying, then forcing them into prostitution, that the full members let him slide on his initiation.

It was Pablo who came up with the idea of selling the "used" girls to prostitution rings in Maryland and the District of Columbia when their own inventory of girls got overfull. This was a wonderful way to keep their flock at a manageable number and also ensure that they remained relatively fresh for the customers. By the time he was turning sixteen Pablo was a child prostitution and sex trafficking entrepreneur.

But with his sixteenth birthday came pressure for him to become a full member of the gang. This would mean killing either a cop or a rival gang member and then submitting to a thirteen-second beat-down by the members of his gang—an event that could easily leave him severely injured.

The pressure was becoming intense. If he didn't comply, they would think that he was disrespecting them. Then, success in prostitution and trafficking or not, he'd risk being hacked to death as an example to others.

In a panic, Pablo hurried to the Marine Corps Recruiting Office on Virginia Beach Boulevard. As he rushed in the door the Gunnery Sergeant looked up and asked, "What can I do for you?"

"I have to join up," said Pablo.

"'Have to'?" asked the Gunny.

"Yeah," said Pablo. "I gotta get out of town as quick as possible."

"And why is that?"

"Uh, I just gotta."

"Son," said the Gunny, "we'd love to have you in the Corps, but you've got to tell me what the rush is."

As Pablo calmed down, he managed to tell the recruiter that he was being pressured to join a gang but didn't want to. He didn't mention that he had been loosely a member for over three years or that he had set up the child sex trafficking business for the local clique. To the recruiter, he was an innocent young man who was trying to escape being forced into a life of crime. "I can't even go home," Pablo said. "They'd find me and take me. Probably even kill me for not joining."

"Well, we can't have that," said the Gunny. "Let's see what we can do."

Pablo spent the afternoon lying his way through the paperwork required for him to join the Marine Corps. It was too late in the day for him to have his recruitment physical, but the Gunny put him up in a dingy motel near the recruiting office and gave him scrip that he could use to buy dinner and breakfast at an adjacent diner. He was waiting at the office door the next morning when the Gunny arrived and was quickly sent by taxi to get his physical done. Fortunately, Pablo did not do drugs, so there was no problem with that. And when the doctor asked him about the "7" and "6" tattoos, he said that they were to celebrate 1776 and the birth of the country. He figured that a loyal Marine would like that.

Arriving back at the recruiting office Pablo finished up with the Gunnery Sergeant, and by seven o'clock he was on a Trailways bus to Parris Island, South Carolina, home of the Marine Corps Recruit Depot for boot camp.

For someone with no experience in discipline, boot camp was rough. Pablo was in good physical condition, so that part was all right. And he was adept at learning to shoot and in hand-to-hand combat. The classroom part, however, was hard. And the need to kowtow to the DIs was worse. Many was the time that he was barely able to restrain himself from punching his DI right in his smug red face, but then he'd remember what was waiting for him if he got sent home to Norfolk, and he sucked it up.

He managed, and after thirteen weeks of boot camp Pablo was a Marine. He had ten days leave coming before reporting in to Camp Geiger in North Carolina for School of Infantry training, but he couldn't go back to Norfolk, so he just moseyed by bus up to Jacksonville, NC, and spent his time hanging around Camp Lejeune and drinking beer in the Jacksonville bars.

The Corps was not too difficult for Pablo, once he got out of training. It was kind of like being in a big gang. They even had the rep of messing up anyone who disrespected them—the Corps. And Pablo loved that.

The recruiter had told Pablo that one of the best moves he could make was to keep putting in for training schools—"it would add to your knowledge, make you more valuable, and keep you out of combat longer." As soon as the School of Infantry was coming to an end Pablo started applying for schools. He knew better than to apply for Recon or Combat Diver schools, but he sent in his application for electronics, communications and, with tongue-in-cheek, military police school. Lo and behold, upon graduating from SOI, he received orders to Ft. Leonard Wood, Missouri, to the Military Police School run by the U.S. Army.

That was how, ultimately, Lance Corporal Pablo Gerena became a Marine Corps Military Policeman. Turned out he loved it. Now he had the authority. Even officers had to listen to him when he was on duty. And enlisted men? Well, they better watch their asses if they messed with MP Gerena. He took no guff. Off duty, Pablo still considered himself a cop. He carried a small .380 caliber pistol in an ankle holster, even though it wasn't authorized, and was always ready and able to break up fights in the bars he frequented off post.

Seeing his willingness to wade into any fight, a crusty old Military Police Staff Sergeant took Pablo aside for some, as he called it, "special training."

"Listen, boy," said the Staff Sergeant, "Why bust your knuckles in a fight?"

"What'll I do, use a baton? Or a chair?"

"Now shut up and listen to me. I'm gonna teach you a little trick. Some call it a 'choke hold,' but it's really just a means of subduing a perp without busting your knuckles or really hurting him. Now watch." He demonstrated on Pablo as he talked.

"First you spin him around." He spun Pablo so his back was to him. "Then you grab him like this."

The Staff Sergeant wrapped his right arm around Pablo's neck so that his neck was nestled in the crook of the Sergeant's elbow.

"Reach up and grab your right wrist with your left hand," he did, "and apply pressure."

Suddenly Pablo felt the pressure on either side of his neck. Five seconds and he was unconscious on the floor.

As he came back to consciousness, Pablo was impressed. Except for a headache, he was fine. "Show me how to do that," he said enthusiastically.

The Staff Sergeant walked him slowly through it again, this time without choking him out. "See? Easy as that. No broken knuckles, and a combatant conveniently unconscious so it's easy to cuff him."

Pablo was excited and looked forward to his next fight so that he could try it out. Officially it was called a Carotid Resistance Control Hold, but the Corps called it a "choke-hold," and it was illegal.

Illegal or not, MP Gerena used his choke hold as often as possible. He used it on base, and he used it subduing bar fights in town. Other MPs wanted to partner with him because he was so quick and good with what they called his "sleeper hold," and it kept them from having to get physical or hurt.

Everything was fine until one night when a fight broke out in the bar where Pablo was drinking. The combatants both had high-and-tight haircuts, so Pablo was sure they were Marines, and in he waded. He grabbed the biggest guy from behind with his sleeper hold, and in ten seconds put him down.

"Oh, man," said the other fighter. "You're in it deep. That's Major Benjamin from Headquarters Company you just choked out. We were just having a friendly fight and now you've stepped in it." Pablo ran, but too many people knew his name, many of whom had received the same treatment from him and wanted payback. The next day he was apprehended by his fellow MPs and hauled "before the mast."

The Captain's Mast, nonjudicial punishment, was over quickly. There were a lot of witnesses, both to the subject fight and to Pablo's love of using the chokehold. The major he'd choked out wanted him in the brig, but his colonel disagreed. He'd been a decent Marine, so they didn't want him to go to the brig, but he was too dangerous to stay in the Corps. His sentence, which he accepted, was a reduction in rank and an 'Other Than Honorable Discharge.' Pablo was a civilian again.

Chapter Fifteen

PAIGE WAS DISSATISFIED with her lack of progress in finding the girl's identification and cause of death. Sure, it wasn't her primary job, but up until now she had been successful. She didn't like the feeling of failure.

There were still some basic tests that she could do. Pulling on her Tyvek suit she took the girl's body out of her refrigerator and slid her onto the stainless-steel embalming table. Of course, a good part of her training had been involved with opening corpses and removing organs in preparation for burial. And, too, she had studied forensics in preparation for her coroner-work, so she was qualified to do what came next.

She went ahead and made a Y-incision to access the girl's lungs. With no obvious wounds Paige at first thought that perhaps the girl had drowned. But when she took out the lungs and examined them there was no water in them. She couldn't have drowned. No bruises, no stab marks or bullet wounds, now no water in her lungs.

Thinking about her forensic training, and the crime procedural shows she had seen on television, she took a large magnifying glass and began to search the girl's body for ... well, anything. Maybe she could find a tiny wound showing a needle prick where either the girl had injected herself with something or someone else had stuck her. She went over the little body looking for something, concentrating on the area between her toes, a favorite spot for drug addicts to use. The crabs and water had done a job on her poor little body but using a large magnifying glass, Paige examined it closely. Nothing. And no word back, yet, on the toxicology screening by the Commonwealth lab in Norfolk.

Although it wasn't really her purview, Paige decided to keep going. Maybe the girl had been strangled. She checked again, but there were no ligature marks on her neck and no bruising. Going further Paige found that the girl's hyoid bone was intact. Although the hyoid bone of a girl this young was still flexible and might not fracture during strangulation, finding it intact further confused Paige. She wanted to be able to give a cause of death, but it didn't look like that was going to happen.

Paige called the sheriff's department. "Hey, y'all, this is Paige Reese. I've done my preliminary on that little girl they found dead down in Cape Charles. I can't come up with a for sure cause of death. There are no wounds, there's no water in her lungs, and there's no sign of strangulation. Guess you'd better call the medical examiner over to Norfolk and have them come take a look." Covering her with a sheet Paige slid the body back into her fridge, placing Bill's six-pack back in place in the cooler.

I really wish he'd not use the body coolers for his beer, she thought.

Paige had a dinner date with Pablo that evening. The Wampler Brothers Band was playing at The Jackspot at Sunset Beach, so they decided to go eat their dinners outside enjoying the band and watching the sunset over the Chesapeake. Paige loved the food at The Jackspot, although it could be pricey. They started out sharing a hot crab dip, made with locally caught crabs. Paige couldn't help but wonder if any of these crabs had been feasting earlier on the little girl in her cooler, but quickly put that out of her mind before she totally lost her appetite.

For the main course, they again shared, this time a basket of steamed clams and locally grown corn-on-the-cob. Paige indulged herself with a frozen Myer's Dark Rum Floater and Pablo drank a Cape Charles Brewing Cobb IPA.

Sated, they sat in the cool evening and talked. When the conversation got around to the murder, Paige told Pablo how she had been totally unable to find a cause of death and how it frustrated her.

"Hey, it ain't no big deal," he responded. "It's just another dead *beaner*. Don't worry your pretty little head about it."

Somehow, he always managed to push Paige's buttons. "NO BIG DEAL?" she said, her voice getting louder. "We've got a dead unknown little girl. We don't know her name. We don't know who killed her. WE DON'T EVEN KNOW HOW SHE DIED!"

Other diners were beginning to look over at them.

"Calm down, Paige," said Pablo, putting his hand on her forearm.

"CALM DOWN?" she shook off his hand. "How can I calm down with this unsolved murder sitting in my cooler? How come you aren't more concerned? Aren't the police supposed to be interested in capturing murderers? Isn't this going to screw up any 'batting average' you might have? What the heck, Pablo? Aren't you a cop? Aren't you a human being? Don't you have a soul?"

"Paige, honey, you're starting to get really personal. And you're making a scene and embarrassing both of us."

"Well—"

He covered her hand with his. "Talk me through it."

"Well, okay. The body of a young girl, around fourteen years old, was found in Cherrystone Creek. The body was wrapped in a fishing net, like an old net from a fish pound, and weighted down with chunks of cinder block. It looked like she had been left in the shallows where the crabs would get rid of the body and the evidence, but she was found before that could happen. After I examined the body, I could find no bruises or wounds, and I haven't heard back from the crime lab about whether there was anything in her blood. I determined that there was no water in her lungs, so she was dead when she went into the creek, and her hyoid bone was intact, indicating that she probably wasn't strangled. She appears to be Hispanic, which would lead us to believe that she is a migrant worker. I managed to take fingerprints, but your search of the data bases came back negative." She paused for a minute, thinking. "When she was found she was dressed in a cheap red gingham dress and white cotton underpants. Her clothes had no tags in them for us to check and were not damaged. Oh! And she showed no bruising around her ... well, her private parts, so there was no apparent rape."

"Did you check to see if her hymen was intact?" asked Pablo.

Paige stammered. "I, uh, well, yes. I checked. It was."

"So, she wasn't shot or stabbed. She wasn't raped. Do you think maybe she was robbed?"

"Pablo, you saw her. There was no way she had anything worth stealing."

"Yeah. Well, if you ask me, she's just a Mexican migrant worker who was probably killed by another migrant worker who's long gone. We ain't got no missing persons paper on her. No one has asked for her or claimed the body. She's just a nobody that nobody cares about. Paige, why waste the time on her? Just let it go."

While she was listing all her findings Paige had thought that maybe Pablo was going to work with her on this. Now she knew he wasn't. He was just trying to talk her out of it.

"I'm contacting the Commonwealth Medical Examiner tomorrow morning to come collect the body and help with the investigation."

"Oh, Paige. Don't get the state people involved. It's not that big a deal. Dammit, girl, you're just going to stir up trouble getting them involved in our business. As the Senior Deputy, I forbid you to do it."

Boom! "YOU FORBID? YOU FORBID? Just who the hell do you think you are?" Paige looked around the restaurant and spotted Donna sitting with her husband Jim at another table. "Donna can you and Jim give me a ride home?" she called.

"Paige," Pablo said quietly.

Paige got up and walked to Donna's table. "I'm sorry, but things have happened, and it looks like I need a ride home."

"Of course," said Donna. "We kinda heard. We'd love to give you a ride. Ready to go?" And together the three walked out of The Jackspot, leaving Pablo to order another beer and nurse his anger and his bruised ego.

Chapter Sixteen

THE NEXT DAY Paige called the Commonwealth's Medical Examiner in Norfolk. It really wasn't her job, or her right, to do so, but she had no faith in the sheriff's department doing it. After working her way through the various levels of telephone bureaucracy she ended up with the Administrative Assistant of the Medical Examiner. The woman sounded intelligent and sympathetic, so Paige poured out the entire tale to her, including how the sheriff's department apparently wanted to just sweep the whole thing under the rug.

"What?" questioned the woman. "That's outrageous. And it's illegal, too. Miss Reese, I'm so glad that you called. I'll fill in the M.E. with the whole story but first I'll arrange for one of our vans to head over and pick the body up from you. Once the body's out of your cooler, there's nothing the sheriff's department can say or do."

"That would be great," enthused Paige. "When can they come over?"

"You just watch your front door. I'm going to send them now. I would imagine they'll be there to collect the body in just over an hour. Please have her in a body bag and ready to go."

"You've got it," said Paige, "and thank you so very much. Will you let me know what you find?"

"Of course. And I'll hurry along the tox screen, too."

"Thank you." Paige hung up the phone.

It was good that the body was in her possession and not at the sheriff's department. Once this was a done deal Pablo could go take a long run off a short pier.

Okay. The Office of the Medical Examiner was going to handle the forensics of the body, but Paige could still do her investigating of the other parts of the case. This was someone's little girl. She had been murdered. And no one in Northampton County seemed to even care. Well, she cared. She was going to do everything she could for the little unknown girl.

"Nott," Paige called up the stairs. "Come help me get the little girl ready for the medical examiner to pick up."

Nott came down the stairs from the apartment. In recent days, through her constant efforts, he was beginning to loosen up and become more verbal. "You're movin' her out?"

"Yes, you know I'm not a real coroner or a medical examiner. I've done everything I can think of, but I still haven't been able to figure out what killed her. The people at the Commonwealth's Medical Examiner's office have the tools and the experience to figure it out."

"Okay. I get that. But we still don't even know who she is. How can we figure out who did her in without even knowing that?"

"Good point," Paige agreed. "That's where we come in."

"We? I ain't no detective."

"I know, but I hope that you and I can figure this thing out just using our common sense."

"What do you want me to do?" asked Nott.

"Well, I think the first thing to do is to look at the obvious. I think we should investigate the high school boys. Do you think you can get their arrest reports?"

Nott replied, "How on earth you expect me to do that? The Sheriff's Department certainly ain't going to help me out. They think I'm the one who committed the murder."

"Yeah," said Paige. "That could present a problem. I'll call my friend Ann Webster Goffigon in the Clerk of Courts office and see if she can help us out. Maybe she can slide me the names and copies of any arrest reports. Let me make a call."

At lunch that day Ann slipped Paige a number of reports from the Sheriff's Department. They were arrest reports for four boys from Northampton High School—Bubba Wilkins, Billy Ray Point, John Marion Heath, and Chris Williams.

"Those are the arrest records," murmured Ann, "but they never got adjudicated."

"Why not?" asked Paige.

"Look at the names," replied Ann. "The last names—they're like a Who's Who of Northampton County. Bubba Wilkins' family owns a huge farm out at Wilkins Beach, Billy Ray Point's family owns a large farm on Savage Neck, John Marion Heath's father was a waterman and now owns a massive clam and oyster farming operation, and Chris Williams' father is a prominent lawyer in Eastville. With their family connections, I'm surprised that we even have this much."

"What all did they do?" asked Paige.

"Well," said Ann, "they never really did anything a judge would sentence them for. At least from what I can tell in these reports. It looks like they just got rambunctious with some of the high school girls, mostly lower-class ones, but never went too far."

"You mean they never killed one?" asked Paige.

"Oh, heavens no!" said Ann. "They were just being boys who let their testosterone get the better of them. I guess they mussed the girls up a little bit, but that's it."

"That's still not right," said Paige. "If they don't get taught a lesson now, who knows where it's going to end? I think maybe I'll have Nott talk with them."

"Nott's still with you?"

"Well, I'm helping them out and keeping an eye on him until this whole mess is put to bed. I don't want the sheriff going back and messing with him anymore."

"Have you got a thing for him?"

Paige laughed. "Of course not. It's more like taking care of a stray cat."

"Just as long as he doesn't curl up on your lap purring," said Ann.

"Now you're starting to sound like Pam." Paige picked up a cheeseburger and French fries for Nott and carried the lunch and the arrest reports back to her office. She sat and looked over the reports while Nott ate his lunch.

"Nott," she said, "I'd like you to talk with these boys and see if they have any ideas about what happened to our unknown little girl. Don't come on real strong. Maybe buy them a beer and chat them up."

"Aren't they underage?"

"Yeah, that's why the beer might be effective in loosening their tongues. Don't get all police-y with them; just befriend them and see what you can learn."

That evening Paige took the case of Billy's cold beer from the body refrigerator in the workroom and gave it to Nott. He took the cold beer, put it in the rusted Ford pickup truck that belonged to the funeral home, and headed out to where he had heard the football team hung out on the beach at Savage Neck Dunes, a state natural area. It was supposed to be closed at sundown, but there were no police or rangers around to enforce it, and it was a good place for a bonfire on the beach. There were about a half-dozen couples there. Someone had brought a bottle of Southern Comfort, and all the kids were getting ... comfortable.

When Nott showed up with his beer he was welcomed as a purveyor of the elixir of life, and the mellowed-out crew was more than happy to accept him ... and his case of brew.

"Hey," one of the boys asked, "aren't you that crazy guy that lives in the old oyster house?"

"Yeah, that's me," answered Nott.

"Why do you live out there all alone?"

Nott proceeded to tell them some tales of his time in the Army and how he got blown up in Fallujah. The boys were fascinated, and soon Nott was fully accepted as one of them.

The breeze was off the water, keeping the mosquitoes away, and the alcohol made it easy to forget about any parental strictures on when to be home. Nott had gone out and bought a second case of beer, and it was around 1:30 in the morning when he started guiding the conversation towards the boys "conquests." By now the girls had left, not wishing to risk fatherly rage, and the boys were drunk enough that they had no inhibitions about talking.

"Man, them was some good lookin' fluff y'all had out here."

"Yeah," said one of the boys, "but they're too much into marryin' before givin' out anything."

"Whaddya mean?" asked Nott.

"Shoot, you know," said another of the boys. "You want to get in their pants, and they'll tease you along and let you get all ready, and then … before you can score, they shut you down. Man, it's painful."

"Well, damn. Whaddya do?"

Another of the boys took a long draw on his can of beer. "Man, there's these cute *Mexicano* girls at school, you know, and you can back them into a corner in the gym or something and cop a feel."

"Don't they complain to the principal?"

"Nah, not usually. They's mostly wetbacks, you know, illegals. They don't want the law looking at them too close or they might get sent back."

"Do they ever go in for any of the rough stuff? Or go all the way?

The boys looked around kind of sheepishly. "Not really," they said. "We'd like to, but ... well, they're beaners, you know. Ya never know whose been there before and what they might have. You don't want to catch anything. Then your parents *would* find out."

"Yeah," Nott said. "That'd suck."

The talk went on from there and circled around to the next football season and whether they'd be able to get scholarships to college. When the beer ran out around 3:15 the party broke up. Stumbling through the soft sand back to the cars was tricky for the boys. Nott had stayed sober, but they finally managed it. Nott was concerned about them making it home safely in their conditions, but there wasn't a lot of traffic this time of night, and none of them had far to go. They drove off, and Nott went back to the beach to clean up the mess of empty cans they had left in the sand. Then he, too, went home. Or at least to his apartment above Reese Funeral Home.

Chapter Seventeen

THE NEXT DAY Nott and Paige talked over what he had learned.

"I don't think they had anything to do with it," he said. "Sure, they're a bunch of horny high schoolers, but I am absolutely certain that if one of them had killed our little unknown girl, first he would have peed his pants, and then he would have run to his daddy to take care of things. I don't think any of them would have had the moxie to try to dispose of the body. And besides, dumping a weighted body in Cherrystone for the crabs is a great way to dispose of a dead victim. It's too devious for these little boys. They would have tried to bury her in the woods. No, I think they are a dead end. You should pardon the pun."

Paige snorted. "Well, heck. I thought they were our best bet. Now what?"

They just sat and thought.

"Nott, you were born in the camp in Machipongo, right?"

"Yeah," he answered cautiously.

"And there're lots of Mexicans that live in the camp there, right?"

"Yeah."

"How about if you dress down and go back to the camp and sniff around?"

"Sniff around? Have you ever been downwind of that place?"

Paige stifled a giggle and thought how Nott seemed to be coming further out of his shell. *He's even making jokes,* she thought.

"You know what I mean," she said. "Do you still know anyone over there?"

"I doubt it. It's been a long time. And … well, that's why they call them 'migrants'. They don't hang around much."

"Even so I think you should give it a try," said Paige. "You may not know anyone, but you know the type of people and how they are. You can fit in and ask questions better than I could."

Nott laughed. "You walk in there with that pretty white face of yours and you won't even see anyone, much less talk with them. Sure. I guess I can go *home*, as it were, and see what I can learn."

That evening after work, dressed in his old camo trousers, a ripped t-shirt and his dirty white waterman's boots Nott wandered into the Machipongo Migrant Camp. A couple of men were sitting on the front stoop of one of the houses, smoking and drinking RC Colas, and Nott walked up to them.

"*Hola*," he greeted them. They just nodded at him. "Pickers?" he asked. Again, they just nodded. "What're they pickin' now?" he asked.

"*Tomates*," replied the one. He was middle-aged with a face so ravaged by the sun you could have planted potatoes in the deep creases. His straw ranch had was fraying at the brim and looked as if it was too holey for the wind to blow it away.

Nott just nodded. "They lookin' for more pickers?"

This time the response was a laconic shrug.

"Mind if I set a piece?"

Another shrug. It was too dark for outside work, and in the still damp air Nott could smell the familiar aroma of frying beans mixed with the miasma of over-stressed sanitary facilities. He sniffed appreciatively. The smells were nostalgic.

"I used to live in this camp. Long time ago. Lived in that house right over there." He pointed with his chin. "Finally signed up for the Army jest to get shed of here."

Noncommittal nods.

"Got blown up over in Fallujah, and now I'm just kinda bummin' 'round. Thought I'd jest check in here to see what's what. See if I knew anyone. You know?"

"Do ya?"

"Huh?"

"Know anybody?"

"Oh," Nott shook his head. "Don't appear so."

An attractive black girl walked down the street towards them with a clipboard in her hand. "Hi," she said.

"Hello *señorita*," said one of the men.

She looked at Nott. "Hi. My name is Glorianna. I'm with the Farm Workers Ministry of the Presbyterian church. You're new here."

Nott nodded. "This time."

"Is there anything I can do for you? I'm here to help."

Nott stood up. "Well, maybe. Can we talk somewhere?"

Glorianna looked a bit concerned, but said, "Sure. Come on. Let's go sit at the picnic table in the grove." Glorianna was "dressed down" to try to fit in with the workers, but whereas their clothes were uniformly torn and dirty, smelling of the sweat of the fields, hers were clean and pressed. It was a good attempt, though.

Once they were seated in the shade Glorianna asked, "Now, what's up?"

"Are there any girls missing?"

Glorianna looked shocked. "What?"

"Are there any girls missing from the camp?"

"Who are you?" she demanded. "Are you some kind of law?"

"No," he replied softly. "I was born in this camp. Now I'm trying to help figure out who killed a little girl and dumped her body in Cherrystone Creek. I found her. The police first thought I did it. Now they know it wasn't me, but they're not real anxious to find out who did it. They don't even know who the little girl is, and they ain't working too hard to find out. So me an' the funeral home lady is tryin' to help."

"With a sad look on her face Glorianna nodded. "Yeah, there're a number of girls has disappeared. And not just from this camp. There're little girls missing from here, from the Concord Camp up to Exmore, the Long Block Camp in Cape Charles and the Carpenter Camp in Capeville."

"My gosh!" exclaimed Nott. "Have the police been notified?"

"No; as you can imagine most of these girls are undocumented. Illegals. Their parents are afraid that if they go to the police they'll get found out and get thrown in jail. That scares them more than losing their girls."

Nott shook his head. "But that's awful!"

"I agree," said Glorianna, "but they can always have another daughter. Lots of them are supporting families back in Mexico. If they lose their jobs here, then the consequences will hurt all the way back there. They just don't want to risk it." A sudden slight breeze ruffled the pages on her clipboard, and Glorianna shifted her grip to hold them down.

"When did this little girl you're talking about disappear?"

"I don't know when she first disappeared, but I found her body last week. So's it got to be recent."

"Describe her."

"Oh, come on! Me? Describe a little girl? She was a little girl."

"How old?"

"Oh, 'bout fourteen I guess."

"How tall?"

"I don't know. As tall as a fourteen-year-old." Nott was getting stressed by all of the questions.

"Okay, calm down. Did she have any scars or tattoos?"

"No, not that I know of."

"What was she wearing?"

"A red gingham dress."

"Anything else?"

"I don't know. I didn't look. I ain't no pervert."

"No, of course not," soothed Glorianna. "It sounds an awful lot like Claudita Briones. She went missing from this camp just ten days ago. We looked everywhere for her. We checked the woods and fields around here and even checked in other camps to see if she got on the wrong bus after work. She never showed up."

"Are her parents still here?"

"No, her father took off as soon as she came up missing. Some said that he must of done something to her. Her mother … well, she pined around for about a week and then she disappeared too. Packed what little she had and took off. Maybe she went after the father."

"Darn," said Nott. "Maybe they was in it together."

"No," replied Glorianna, "I knew Claudita and her mother. She was a sweet little girl, and her mother loved her very much. She wouldn't have done anything to hurt her. That's what broke her heart when Claudita disappeared. That's why her mother, left so that she wouldn't be reminded of what all she had lost here."

Sadly, Nott agreed with her.

Well, he had achieved some success. The little girl was probably Claudita Briones, an undocumented migrant worker who most recently had been living in the Machipongo Migrant Camp.

But more upsetting was the discovery that Claudita's disappearance was apparently just one of several little girls, vanished from the labor camps. He had to get back and talk this over with Paige.

Chapter Eighteen

"OH, GOD, NO!" cried Paige in anguish when Nott told her about the other missing little girls. "No, Nott. How many?"

"I don't really know. They never reported them to the sheriff, so there's nothing official."

"But ... but, you're sure?"

"Yeah. I was talkin' to this woman who helps the farm workers for the Presbyterian Church. She's the one told me. She works in all of the camps in the county so she kinda knows what's goin' on."

Paige couldn't help it. She cried, "Those poor babies! And their mothers. Think about how their mothers must feel. To not know!"

Paige was feeling unaccustomedly maternalistic, thinking about the missing little girls, and couldn't stop sobbing. Nott stood there awkwardly, not knowing what to do.

He wanted to pat her shoulder but was afraid to touch her. "There, there, Paige. It's okay. It'll be okay. Please stop crying." He had a tear in his own eye, now.

Slowly Paige brought herself under control. "Nott, we've got to find out what's been happening to these little girls over here. No one else is doing anything. We've got to do it!"

"Okay," he said hesitantly. "But I don't know what we can do that the law can't."

"But that's the point. The law won't do anything. Just like with our little Claudita. They're not real to them. Not really humans. They're just tools that are used to farm the land. Like tractors. And there's such a supply of them it really doesn't matter if one or two get lost. If they won't do anything, then we have to."

"Well, there's really only one person screwing everything up—your boyfriend."

"He's not my ... well, I guess he sort of is. But it's nothing serious. And if he won't do his job with these missing girls, then we'll have to do it for him."

The next night was a fund-raiser fish fry at the Cheriton Volunteer Fire Department. This was a regular event and Paige always enjoyed not only the fish but the fellowship. It was a very popular event, and good to show her support for the community.

Nott attended with her, and as could be expected was rather shy. He wasn't monosyllabic when spoken to, however, and didn't pull his head down into his shoulders like a turtle. He just didn't initiate any conversations.

Birdie came in, saw Nott, and made a beeline for him. "Why, Nott. How handsome you look."

Nott wasn't quite ready for this. "Hi, Miss Birdie."

"Are you here with Paige?"

He nodded. "Yeah, I'm still living upstairs at her business until the sheriff says I can go back to my own place."

"That little shack of yours?" Birdie asked, surprised.

"Well, yeah. That's my home."

Birdie sniffed somewhat disdainfully. "Well…"

Paige joined them. "Miss Birdie, you see a lot of people at Rayfield's and have a good idea of what all's goin' on. Have you heard anything about other little girls goin' missing?"

"Heavens no, Paige. What do you mean? I'm sure the sheriff or Sergeant Heath could answer that better than I could," Miss Birdie exclaimed.

"No, ma'am," said Paige, "I'm talking about little girls who've gone missing and not been reported to the police."

"Not been reported?" asked Miss Birdie, confused.

"From what I've been able to gather there's a number of farm girls, migrant workers, who have disappeared over the last little while. Their parents tend to be undocumented—"

"You mean illegal?"

"Yes, and so they are afraid to go to the authorities for fear they'll get themselves in trouble. I guess they try to look as best they can, and then give up or move on."

"How horrible," exclaimed Miss Birdie. "I can't imagine."

"No."

Just then Sergeant Heath came in and Paige went over to talk with him. Heath was what you'd picture in your imagination of a small-town police officer. His uniform barely contained his large body, and his equipment-laden utility belt's buckle was completely hidden by an overhanging paunch. But he was good natured, appreciated the tourists who were bringing so much money into his little city, and was generally appreciated, if not loved.

"Good evening, Sergeant Heath," Paige said pleasantly.

"Paige! How're you doin', young lady?" he responded. "How's that house guest of yorn workin' out? He kill any of your customers yet?" Heath chuckled at his own joke—killing funeral home customers.

"No, Sergeant, and I haven't caught him sleeping in any of the body coolers, either," was her response. She waved Nott over, and he came cautiously.

"You remember Sergeant Heath, Nott?"

Nott's speech temporarily left him, and he muttered an "Mmmph," as he nodded his head. Heath looked at him amused by the effect he had on the man.

"Sergeant, if you've a moment you could spare me, I've some things I'd like to ask," said Paige.

"Well, just let me get a plate of fish and corn before it's all gone," said Heath, and wandered off to the food tables where the firefighters were serving. When his plate was full, he went and sat down at a table away from Paige and Nott.

Oh no you don't, thought Paige. *You're not brushing me off that easy.*

Grabbing Nott's arm, she maneuvered him over to the table where Sergeant Heath was studiously ignoring them.

"So, Sergeant Heath," started out Paige as the officer sipped his sweet tea. "Can we talk?"

"Doesn't look like you're gonna leave me alone 'til we do," he grumbled.

"Oh, c'mon, Sergeant," Paige chided. "Don't you wanna talk to me?"

"What do you wanna know?" he asked.

"I heard that this isn't the first little girl to go missing."

"What? Who told you that?" sputtered Heath.

"Oh, it's just some gossip I've picked up," said Paige. "Is there anything to it?"

"Paige, you know better than to believe gossip, don't ya?"

"That's why I'm asking you. I figured you could give me the straight story."

"Well, I've heard some stories, too, but I don't put much stock in them. And ain't no one come in and filed a missin' person with us. No official report, no missin' person."

"Yeah, but they told me that the missing girls are undocumented so they're afraid to go to the police."

"Who told you? Who's been feedin' you this?"

"Oh, just folks."

"Well, folks ought to be more careful 'bout tales they tell. Spreadin' false rumors can get people scared. And we don't want to scare our citizens or our visitors, do we?"

Paige nodded her head noncommittally. She didn't want to get roped into this. "Well, Sergeant, I've eaten my fill, and it's time to corral Nott and head back up the road."

"Nott? So that freeloader's still bunkin' with you?"

"Oh, for pity's sake. Talk about spreading rumors. No! He is not *bunking* with me. He is staying in the apartment at the Home and I am staying at my apartment at the beach."

"Why?"

Paige did a double take. "Why? Why aren't we staying together? What do you take me for, Sergeant Heath? You've got a lot of damn gall to make a statement like that. If that's the direction your dirty mind takes you, you shouldn't be allowed around nice people. You ought to have your mind washed out with lye soap."

Heath stepped back from Paige's tirade.

"Well, I—"

"You what?" she demanded.

"C'mon, Paige. You know I didn't mean it like that."

"Do I? It seems that you and Pablo and the others think that a woman is only good for two things. Right, Heath? Keep 'em barefoot and pregnant? I'll tell you what—I'm going to find out who killed that little girl. And I'm going to find out what happened to those other missing girls, too. While you're sitting around eating donuts."

"Paige, wait! What other girls? You got any proof?"

"Oh," she sneered. "Didn't know that there's a bunch of young girls gone missing over the last little while, huh?"

"Okay, Paige. Let's get serious. What are you talkin' about?"

"According to the lady from the Presbyterian Church that works with the farm laborers there are several more missing girls from the various camps that no one is looking for. No one official, that is."

"Dang. Paige, honestly, this's the first I heard of it. Why didn't anyone file a report?"

Paige calmed down a little. "According to the lady, they are probably undocumented, so their parents are afraid of the police ... afraid that if they make a fuss they'll be found out and arrested."

Heath nodded. "Yeah, they don't realize that we ain't the border patrol. If they break the law, we'd hold them on a detainer, but on something like this ... doggone it, Paige. Don't they realize that we want to help them find their kids?"

"No," said Paige, "I suppose not. I suppose the police where they come from aren't quite so understanding, so they just don't trust anyone in authority. Are you going to help me?"

"I'll do what I can. If it's not in the city limits, though, then it's the county's jurisdiction. Can't you get Pablo to help out?"

Paige snorted. "No, he's not interested. So, I'll keep on doing it without his help. Thanks, Heath. I'll let you know if there's anything you can do."

With that Paige went to round up Nott and head back up the road to Eastville. At least she now had something of an ally. Hopefully, he'd be of some help.

Chapter Nineteen

IT WAS FORTUNATE that the funeral business was slow at the moment. She still needed to keep her face in front of people for her sales recognition, but the present dearth of actual funerals gave Paige a fair amount of free time to pursue her investigation. She enlisted Nott's help.

Nott was coming more and more out of his shell. The more time he spent around people, non-threatening welcoming people, the better he was able to cope. Paige took him with her to church each Sunday. The early service was a contemporary service, and Nott seemed to enjoy the more participative worship. She took him to Wednesday night Bible study, to her CBES meetings—pretty much wherever she went. Although he said that he missed his shack on Cherrystone Creek, he did seem to be warming to a more urban-ish lifestyle.

With the case of the little girl weighing on her mind, Paige decided that they needed to expand their investigation. The first thing that she did was to take Nott with her and cross the Bridge-Tunnel to Portsmouth in order to contact the Presbytery of Eastern Virginia's Migrant Ministry. Back on The Shore, she had been getting the run-around from so many people she wanted to meet with them face-to-face and press her questions. That was where she was able to learn the name of her little girl, Claudita, and she hoped that they could shed more light on the whole missing girl problem.

Fortunately, Glorianna, the woman Nott talked to, was there and remembered Nott and his search for Claudita.

"Hello, Nott," greeted Glorianna. "Have you had any more luck finding who hurt our little Claudita?"

Paige stepped forward. "Glorianna? Hi, I'm Paige Reese from Eastville. I'm sort of the coroner over there, and Nott's been working with me trying to find out who killed our little girl. Nott said you told him that Claudita's not the only little girl to go missing?"

Glorianna motioned them into a little office. "Do you want some coffee?" she asked.

"No, thanks. We're pretty much coffee'd out. But what can you tell us about missing girls?"

Glorianna took on a sad and worried expression. "Paige, I work in all 96 of the Northampton County labor camps. We try to provide soap and sunscreen and diapers and other hygiene items to all of the workers who need them. We have a Hunger Ministry, too, where we try to make sure that the babies and kids get enough nutritional food so that they can grow up healthy. It's really an uphill battle, but with the Lord's help, and plenty of donations from the people, I think we're making a difference."

"Yes," said Paige. "All of that is wonderful, but what about the missing children?"

"Oh, yes. The little girls. Well, mostly they disappear from camps south of Accomack County. Machipongo, Capeville, Exmore…"

"But where do they go? Do they ever turn up? How many of them have gone missing?"

Glorianna replied, "Well, they are all little girls around thirteen to fifteen. They just … don't come home one day. It's been going on for a couple of years, now, but the numbers aren't large—maybe two or three a year—and they don't get reported to the authorities because they are almost all illegals. Oh, their families search for them. They scour the fields and the woods, but there's never a trace. Finding Claudita's body … well, that's the first time anyone's showed up once they went missing."

"Have you any guess about who's takin' them?" asked Nott.

"No," said Glorianna. "If it were only one time, I'd think maybe they were walking on the highway and someone, maybe a trucker, stopped and took them. But I just don't know."

The three of them sat there, just thinking.

"Dammit," said Paige. "Someone's got to know something. Someone's gotta care about what's going on."

"Only the three of us, right now," said Glorianna.

"Whaddya s'pose happens to them?" asked Nott.

Glorianna looked very glum and disturbed. "Nott, these are all young girls. Just beginning to bud, if you know what I mean. I knew a couple of them, and they were really pretty, for being babies."

Nott nodded his head, not fully understanding where Glorianna was going with this.

"It's pretty horrible to think about, but I think they are being trafficked—forced into prostitution."

Nott was horrified. "But they're just little girls!" he exclaimed.

"Yeah," said Glorianna, "but there're people that want 'em that young. And are willing to pay extra for it."

"That's sick," he said.

"It is," she agreed. "People like that ought to be ... well, I can't say it in nice company. But you know what I mean."

"Yeah, with a dull fish knife," said Paige.

"Well, who's doin' it?" asked Nott.

Paige nodded. She wondered, too.

"I don't know," said Glorianna. "But if it is for sex trafficking, then maybe the FBI would know something. That's federal. It's not the sex, *per se*, but forcing them to do it is called 'involuntary servitude.' It's slavery. It just happens to be for sex, which is actually a state crime. But that's where you might want to start."

"The FBI?" asked Nott. "Are they around here?"

Glorianna nodded. "The Norfolk Field Office is located in Chesapeake. The Eastern Shore is under their jurisdiction."

Thanking Glorianna, Nott and Paige went back to her car. "Now what?" Nott asked.

"I guess we go to the FBI Field Office," Paige replied, as they drove off.

THE FBI FIELD Office was located in a three-story modern building bristling with antennae. As they drove up to the gate an armed guard stopped their car, and Paige began to wish she had called ahead for an appointment.

"I need to see an FBI-man," she said to the guard.

He smiled indulgently. "Well, ma'am, we've got a bunch of *Special Agents* here, is there anyone in particular?"

Crap, thought Paige. "No, I don't know any of the agents. I need to ask about a crime ... about missing little girls."

"In Norfolk?"

"No, over on the Eastern Shore. There's a body, too."

"A body, ma'am?"

Paige wasn't getting anywhere. "My name is Paige Reese and I'm the coroner in Northampton County. We found the body of a young girl there, and my inquiries so far indicate that there are a number of other girls missing."

"Have their bodies shown up?"

Paige was trying hard to control her temper. Her knuckle turned white as she gripped the steering wheel and her jaw grew stiff. She spoke between clenched teeth. "No, Mr. Gate Guard, only the one body. But since there are others missing as well, I thought I should talk with someone."

"Did you talk with the local sheriff?"

Now she had reached her boiling point. "Listen: I'm not going to go through the whole 'I pay your salary with my taxes' routine. I am making an official report that there is something going on with young girls on the Eastern Shore and demanding to be able to talk with someone—someone other than a gate guard—about it."

The guard was taken aback. He retreated into his guard shack and made a phone call. He came back to the car. "Yes, ma'am. Special Agent Hannegan will talk with you. Please park your car over there in the visitor's lot, and the Special Agent will meet you at the front door."

Paige icily replied, "Thank you."

As they approached the front door of the building it opened and Special Agent Hannegan came out to greet them with two visitor's passes. "Please come on in. We can talk in the first-floor conference room. It's not in use at the moment."

In Paige's eyes, Special Agent Tim Hannegan was beautiful. He was just over six-feet tall and slender with almost black hair turning just a little gray at the temples. He was probably in his late thirties, and a quick habitual glance showed her no wedding ring nor suntan band where one had been. And his eyes. His eyes were just about the bluest turquoise that Paige had ever seen, and as he smiled, she fell right into them.

Nott didn't seem as impressed but tagged along behind as Hannegan led them to the glassed-in conference room.

"Now, then, Miss Reese was it?"

Paige nodded.

"What can the Bureau help you with?"

Paige took a deep breath and gathered herself, then retold the entire story of Claudita's body being found and her findings that missing girls, migrant farmworkers, were apparently not uncommon on the Eastern Shore. Hannegan was attentive, not interrupting and jotting down notes on a yellow legal pad.

"And why are you telling me this instead of your own sheriff?"

Paige recounted to Special Agent Dreamboat how she had tried to get Senior Deputy Gerena interested in the case, but how he had blown her off. "He seems to think that because the little girl…"

"Claudita?"

"Yes, because Claudita is probably undocumented, and no one has bothered to report her missing, that she's a non-person. Not worth worrying about. And I don't understand it. He's Hispanic too. Shouldn't he be a bit more sympathetic?"

"Is he undocumented, too?"

"No. He was born in Norfolk. Grew up in Grandy."

"Okay, so you think there's an ongoing crime, but you can't get the proper authorities interested in it. Right?"

Paige nodded.

"And you, sir?" Hannegan looked at Nott. "What's your part in all of this?"

"I found the body."

"Ah," said Hannegan.

"And they first tried to charge me with her murder. But I had nothing to do with it."

"So originally, they were interested in the little girl's murder, then not?"

"Yeah," said Paige. "Once they were convinced that it couldn't have been Nott, they said that it was an unsolvable 'death by unfortunate mishap,' and stopped looking"

"And the other missing girls?"

"As I said, no one has filed any missing person reports, so the Sheriff's Office doesn't see them. No paperwork, no crime."

Chapter Twenty

"SO, THIS IS kind of personal for you?" asked Hannegan. "You seem really caught up in it."

Paige had to think for a moment. "Well, I've never been maternal, but this little unknown girl has touched my heart. She's so small and so innocent, and it seems that nobody cares about her. No one cares that she's dead and no one cares who killed her. That got me first. Then when I found out that she's only one missing girl of several … I … it just got to me. I don't have any kids. I've got a brother, but I wouldn't mind if he went missing. But these little girls … they are all someone's daughters. Someone loved them. And now they just disappear, and their mothers don't know where, and they are afraid to ask, and so they just become … like, non-persons. If they're illegals, then there's no record that they were ever here, and if they are dead but never found, there's no record that they left.

It's frightening. Just stop and think—what if you just disappeared, and all the paperwork that said you were here disappeared, and all of the pictures of you faded away? It sounds like a horror movie."

"Wow!" said Nott. "You really have got caught up."

Paige half-smiled sheepishly. "I'm sorry. I didn't mean to go on like that. It's just that I get so mad thinking about it all."

"I understand," said Hannegan, and Paige felt the blood rush to her face and neck with his recognition.

"So, what can we do?"

"Without official missing person complaints there's only so much that I can do through the Bureau," said Hannegan. "You know how governmental agencies are—by the book. Got to follow protocols. And the Bureau is right up there with the worst of them. All you actually have is one body and a bunch of hearsay."

"Hearsay!"

"Now calm down, Paige. Think about it. That's what it is. You don't have any other names, you don't have any paperwork, you don't have any complainants … hearsay."

"But—"

"I'm not saying that I don't believe you. It's just that the Bureau won't get involved until I can provide them with something concrete. We've got the Innocence Lost Initiative and the Human Trafficking Task Force, but they just won't do anything until we have a solid complaint."

"What can we do, then?" asked Paige querulously.

"Paige, I'd suggest that you and Nott go back over to The Shore and just keep your ears open. And let me know if you come up with anything solid. But do not, I repeat, do not pretend that you are a detective and get involved any further in this. You do that and you'll probably mess up the investigation and might even get yourself hurt."

Paige was beginning to heat up again. "Investigation? What investigation is there for me to mess up? You're not going to do anything because 'the Bureau won't get involved' until I or someone presents them with a finished case, and Gerena isn't going to do anything 'cause he's too lazy, and Sergeant Heath isn't going to do anything 'cause 'it's not in his jurisdiction.' So, what is there for me to mess up?"

It's a good thing she's so pretty when she's pissed, thought Hannegan, *'cause she sure seems to stay that way.* "Paige, I'll be doing something, and I don't need you muddying the waters. And I certainly don't need you getting yourself hurt. So, you and Nott go back to Eastville and don't do anything more than keep your ears open. Okay? Okay, Nott?"

Nott nodded his head. Paige just stood there fuming.

"Where's the body now?" asked Hannegan.

"I had to ship it to the Commonwealth Medical Examiner's lab," replied Paige.

"Well, y'all get back across The Bay and let me see what we can do with this."

Nott took a stiff Paige by the elbow and steered her back out of the building and to their car. "Damn, I hate to be treated like a helpless little girl," Paige muttered.

"Well, that's kinda what you are," said Nott quietly.

"What?" Paige shouted, rounding on Nott.

Nott put his hands up in a defensive posture. "Whoa, wait a minute! I'm just saying that you *are* a girl and you—we—really don't have any jurisdiction in this."

"I have jurisdiction! I'm the coroner."

"No, you're not. Not really. You're just a volunteer who gets the bodies first."

"Well ... I..."

"C'mon, Paige. I appreciate everything you've done for me, and I appreciate what you are trying to do for the girls. I'll help. I believe in you. But you've got to recognize and admit that we are flying without any safety net of authority."

By now they were driving over the Bridge-Tunnel. It was a clear and sunny day, but there was a good breeze blowing, and the occasional gusts rocked the car. As they cleared Fisherman Island and saw the lights of the Mallard Cove Marina complex Paige let out a sigh and said, "Let's see if Sergeant Heath will give us any official help. At least he believes what we're saying."

Using her cell phone Paige called the Cape Charles Police Department and found that Sergeant Heath was eating his supper at the Mallard Cove Beach Bar. Taking one of the numerous crossovers through the highway median Paige executed a U-turn and drove them back south to Mallard Cove.

When they arrived some of the charter fleet had just returned and the dock was bustling with fishermen having their pictures taken with catches, boat deckhands cleaning and filleting fish, others washing down their boats with freshwater hoses, and calls for "beer!" The cooks from Mallard Cove Restaurant were there also, dickering with the fishermen who wanted to sell their catch. All-in-all it seemed to be a happy bunch.

Inside the bar, looking out at the hubbub, sat Sergeant Heath. He was nursing a Smith Island Stout from the Cape Charles Brewing Company and nibbling on a basket of Old Bay seasoned potato chips. When he saw Paige and Nott he waved them over.

Rising slightly, he said, "Howdy, Miss Paige. And is this young man Nott? Damn, boy, you clean up pretty well."

Nott flushed a bit but said nothing. He was still wary of Heath after he had arrested him for the little girl's death. They joined Heath at the table.

"Where you kids been?" he asked.

While Nott sat mutely, Paige told Heath about their trip to the Presbyterian Migrant Ministry in Portsmouth where they learned that Claudita was not the only little girl gone missing from the Eastern Shore labor camps. Then she told him about their visit to the FBI in Chesapeake.

"Damn, girl! The FBI? What are you trying to start?"

"Sergeant Heath, I'm not trying to cause any trouble," said Paige. "But you know that Pablo isn't interested in investigating the little girl's death, and if he isn't interested in investigating when he has a body, he sure isn't going to investigate when all he has is rumors of missing girls. He just isn't."

"Well, with the lack of any evidence—"

"That's what the FBI agent said. Without anything concrete to go on, they won't even open an investigation. He more-or-less patted me on the head and told me to go home and be a good girl."

Nott leaned over to Paige and said, *sotto voce*, "Didn't look to me like it was your head he was thinkin' of pattin'." Paige gasped and drove a sharp elbow into Nott's ribs. Nott laughed and groaned at the same time.

"Huh?" said Heath.

"Nothing," snapped Paige, as she looked daggers at Nott. She didn't appreciate his humor, right now, but she had to admit it had him smiling. That was a slight victory, even if it had to come at her expense.

"Well, Paige, just what do you expect me to do?" asked the police sergeant.

"I don't know," moaned Paige. "Agent Hannegan told us to just keep our ears open and stay out of it. But I can't just let it go. I have to do something … something to help the little girl that Nott found and something for the other little girls who have gone missing. But what?"

The waitress came over. Sergeant Heath ordered another stout and another basket of Old Bay Chips and Paige ordered a glass of the house red wine, knowing that it was a merlot from the Chatham Vineyards just up the road. Nott settled for a bottle of water.

"Tell you what," said Heath. "I know some of the farmers that use labor from the Capeville and Cheriton camps; some from the Eastville camp, too. Why don't I just casually ask them what they know? See if I can get anything from them. They're good ol' boys who have good relationships with their farm-workers, maybe they can add somethin' in."

"That'd be good," Paige said, and Nott nodded. "And I'll follow up with the Commonwealth's Medical Examiner. The full autopsy and tox screen must be back by now."

"You know, I could go back undercover at some of the other camps," said Nott. "Sergeant Heath, you sure can't go in there askin' questions. And Paige, there's no way you can pass for a farmworker. I been there, done that. I'll talk with the people there and see what's what."

"Sounds like we got a plan," said Paige, as they finished off their drinks and headed out. As she was walking to the parking lot Paige heard a painfully loud engine roar. Turning back to the marina she could see that it was Pablo pulling in with his Cigarette boat, racing the engine in neutral to get all the attention he could. She shook her head at his childishness and turned away.

Chapter Twenty-One

SEEING PABLO HEADING in with his Cigarette boat Heath turned away from the parking lot and walked on down to the dock. He shooed away the dock boy, catching and tying off Pablo's mooring lines for him.

"What's the weather looking like?" called Pablo. "Do I need to double up any lines?"

"No, looks to be nice for the next few days," answered Heath. "C'mon ashore and I'll buy ya a beer."

Together they walked up to the Mallard Cove Beach Bar and took a table in the corner.

"Looks like the fisherpersons done a good job," commented Pablo.

"Yeah, they been comin' in for a while," replied Heath. "Bunch of them had black drum and even some tautog to sell to the cook. If you're hungry you oughta be able to get a really fresh fish sandwich right about now."

The waitress came over and they both ordered beers.

"Ya ever do any fishin' off that thing of yours?" asked Heath, nodding toward the bright yellow go-fast boat.

"Naw. I ain't about to get fish guts on that beauty. I want seafood I'll just buy it. Besides, sitting there waiting for something to bite is a little like lying in the grave waitin' for the first shovel of dirt. Boring as death itself."

"Oh, I don't know. It's a good way to unwind. Shoot, some of these summer days the tourists down in town are such a pain. If I didn't have fishing to look forward to, the quiet of just sittin' in the sun with a beer and a pole, I'd probably shoot one. 'Specially the Yankees from New York."

Pablo laughed at that one. "Yeah, they can really be a trial."

"Speakin' of trial," said Heath, "y'ever get anyone for the murder of that little Mex girl?"

"The one you arrested that homeless guy for? Nott?"

"Yeah, whatever came of that?"

"Shoot, Heath. Nothin' t'all. Took us forever jest to figure out who she was, and then when it was obvious the bum couldn't have done it, I jest kind of put it over in the open-but-cold pile. Ain't no one ever reported her missing, so ain't no one pushing for an investigation. I gots enough other stuff to keep me busy without doing make-work on a nothing case like that."

"But didn't Paige tell you about the other missing worker girls?"

"Paige," Pablo snorted. "She's cute and all, but she don't know anything about missing girls. She's just bleedin' over this one dead body ... and she doesn't even know her! Naw, I can't get myself all wrapped around the axle over what Paige thinks."

"But aren't you two—"

"Nah. She won't come across. She's an okay date once in a while, but I'm sure not going to let her tell me what to do."

"Pablo, I've been a cop for a long time. Probably as long as you've been in long pants. I know you're Senior Deputy, and in another department, but ... well, Pablo, I sure don't want to try to tell you how to do your job, but this is a murder. Sure, it's only a farm-worker and apparently there's no one looking for her, but do you really feel okay with putting it in your cold case file?"

Pablo wasn't happy with Heath's criticism. "Old man, who the hell do you think you're talkin' to? I did plenty of investigatin' in the Corps. I know when a case has possibilities and when it's a waste of time. This one's a waste. Got it?"

Heath looked at him. "Son, why're you so set on burying this case? It's a murder. That's about as big as you can get. I just don't understand. Are you involved with this somehow?"

Pablo's face turned a bright crimson as he shouted at Heath, "What the hell do you mean 'involved'?" He leaned forward, inches away from Heath's face.

Heath tried to back away, but Pablo grabbed his shirt front and pulled him in close. He smelled the beer on Pablo's breath, and felt the spit as Pablo yelled in his face. "Listen, you old sack of guts, don't you ever say something like that again ... to me or anyone else. You think you're so much better than me." He lowered his voice to a conspiratorial whisper. "If I hear you've said this to anyone else, I'll tell them 'bout the time I caught you and that underage little girl having sex in the dunes out to Savage Neck Park. That'll cost you your job and maybe even end you up in jail. *My* jail. I'll make sure of it."

Sergeant Heath broke free and staggered back. He could feel the blood drain from his face and felt he might pass out. "That was years ago," said Heath. "And she told me she was nineteen."

Pablo smiled with evil satisfaction. "Yeah, well that won't matter when I show the judge the signed statement I got from the girl."

"You what?" asked Heath, his eyes bursting from his head.

"Yeah, after I let you go I had her hand-write a statement about you and her having sex, and about her being only fifteen years old. It was my deal for letting her go and not telling her parents. She was happy to do it, and I've been keepin' it in my safe ever since."

Heath staggered back into a chair. Tears were beginning to fill his eyes.

"Come to think of it," mused Pablo, "maybe you're the one. You like the little girls, maybe you're the one involved with them going missing. You think?"

Heath raised his hands as if to ward off a blow and staggered back from Pablo. Turning, he raced out the door to his patrol car in the parking lot. He could hear Pablo's mocking laughter coming from the bar as he slammed his patrol car into gear and spun gravel all over as he raced away from Mallard Cove Marina.

Back inside Pablo sat back down, drained his beer and ordered another. "Let me have one of those fish cake sandwiches I've heard so much about," he told the waitress. He leaned back in his chair and gazed out over the moored boats gently bobbing in the waters of the Chesapeake.

Chapter Twenty-two

THE OFFICIAL REPORT from the medical examiner went to the Sheriff's office, and Paige went over to request a copy.

"Well, Miss Paige," said the desk sergeant, "since you ain't official, I don't know that I can give you a copy of an official Commonwealth's report."

Paige's Irish got up, again. "What do you mean? I was the first one to post the body. You've never even seen her. I'm the one that insisted she be sent to the Commonwealth's Medical Examiner. And you're telling me that I don't have the right to see what the M.E. found?"

"Well, Miss Paige, you know how privacy laws work nowadays. Don't want to get the sheriff in any trouble or anything."

"THE GIRL IS DEAD! I had her body lying on a slab in my lab. I took a magnifying glass and examined every square inch of her. And now you're telling me that you can't let me see the report because of 'privacy laws'?"

He looked sheepishly at his desk, pushing the pencils around on it to get lined up with the stapler and desk calendar.

"Get me a copy of that report now before I lose my temper completely and jump across this desk and beat you with that stapler you keep fidgeting with."

"Well, umm, yes ma'am. I'll jest clear it with the Senior Deputy and then I'll get it for you."

"I don't care if you have to clear it with your mother. If I don't have a copy of that report in five minutes you're going to see some real havoc. Got it?"

The desk sergeant hustled off. Normally a session like this would make Paige feel really good. She hated when someone treated her like a helpless little girl, and that happened a lot over in this agrarian society. So, when she popped off like this and sent an older man scurrying to do her bidding, she usually got a feeling of vengeful satisfaction.

This time she was simply too angry. Sure, she wasn't a police officer or even an official coroner, but they'd asked for her help when they first got the body. And now that she'd given them her help, they were blowing her off. Well, she simply wasn't going to stand for it, and they'd better be fully aware of that. This was *her* case, and she was going to follow it. And if they couldn't do anything then, by golly, she was going to solve it.

The desk sergeant came out of the back with an embarrassed smile and a large manila envelope. "Here you are, Miss Paige. Glad to be of service. Jest sign this receipt for it and that's it."

Paige signed the receipt, took the envelope, nodded at the desk sergeant as she left the office. Once outside she did give a slight smile and a slight sigh of satisfaction that once again she had put an overbearing idiot in his place.

Back in her office, Paige telephoned her friends Pam, Donna and Ann Webster. "You want to meet for lunch?" she asked.

"Sure," they answered, and they arranged to meet at the Machipongo Trading Post out on the highway.

Paige was already sitting at a table, drinking an iced cafe con leche when the others wandered in. On the table in front of her was a stack of papers and photographs, and she was reading through them.

"Wat'cha got?" asked Pam as they walked to the table and pulled out chairs.

"We finally got the official report from the Medical Examiner. I'm just going through it."

Donna said, "Can we see it?"

"No," said Paige. "I can't let you read it but let me read some points from it for you. Then you can help me brainstorm."

The other two nodded their heads anxiously.

"Well, just like I said when I did my examination, they didn't find any outward signs of injuries. There weren't any gunshot wounds or knife cuts, no bruises. Oh! This is interesting: there were no ligature marks anywhere."

"What are ligature marks?" asked Pam.

"Ligature marks are the bruises and wounds you get when you're strangled with a cord or something. They can really tell a lot—what kind of thing they used to strangle you, whether you were hung or just strangled…"

"*Just* strangled," snorted Ann.

"They'll indicate whether someone actually wrapped his hands around your throat to strangle you or if he used a cord of some kind. The body had no ligature marks at all on her neck."

Paige held her wrists out in front of her. "She didn't have any ligature marks on her wrists, either."

"What does that mean?"

"Ligature marks on her wrists would have indicated that she had been tied up. There's no sign of that. So, she was almost certainly dead when she got thrown into Cherrystone."

She kept reading. "Of course, that's all on the surface. If she was strangled, she'd show petechial hemorrhaging in her eye…"

"Pet-what?" asked Ann.

"Petechial hemorrhaging. When someone dies of strangulation the little blood vessels in the eye burst and you can see the red bleeding in the eyeball itself."

"Did she have that?" asked Donna.

"Can't tell," responded Paige.

"Why not?"

"The crabs got her eyes."

"I was going to have crab salad for lunch," said Donna. "Think I'll go with a spinach salad instead." Pam swallowed hard.

Paige flipped a sheet in the report. "That's all the surface stuff. They checked her lungs and they didn't have any water in them, so she didn't drown."

"That's good," said Donna. "Drowning really scares me."

"Now, when they examined her neck internally they found that her hyoid bone was still intact."

"Okay," said Pam. "Here you go again with your fancy terminology. Her what bone?"

"Her hyoid bone," said Paige. "It's a little bone just above the voice-box and below the tongue. It isn't always certain, but if it is broken it usually means that someone was strangled. Her's wasn't broken."

"So she wasn't strangled?" said Donna, questioningly.

"Let me read further. Hmmm. Well, they did further investigation in her neck and found deep tissue damage. The carotid arteries were crushed." Looking up Paige said, "That's what killed her."

The other two just looked at her.

Paige put her index fingers on either side of her neck. "The carotids carry blood to the brain. Crush them, and you die. Pretty quickly. Death from anoxic encephalopathy," she said, reading from the report. "We'd think of strangulation as killing us by cutting off our air. That still takes a while to happen. This kind of strangulation cut off the blood to the little girl's brain, and that's what killed her."

The three of them sat there quietly for a few minutes thinking about what they'd just learned.

"Did she have any drugs in her system?" asked Donna.

Paige referred to the report. "Nope, tox screen came back completely clean."

Again, they sat and thought.

"Now what?" asked Pam.

Paige shook her head. "Well, it's officially a homicide, now. Of course, when you find a dead body wrapped in fishnet weighted down in the creek there's not much question. But once the M.E. says it, it's in the paperwork. Sheriff's gotta do something now. I'll talk with Pablo and see what's going to happen. I'll let you know. Just don't tell anyone I told you about the report, for Pete's sake."

They shook their heads "no," and the four left for their respective offices. Paige had a challenge in front of her, but first she was going to talk with Nott.

Chapter Twenty-Three

"NOTT, WHAT DO you think we should do now?" asked Paige.

"Well, Paige, I've kind of just been following your lead. I don't know anything about this stuff. I can run a line of crab pots, but I don't know nothin' about bein' a detective."

"I know," said Paige, "but we can't stop now."

They were having supper at Nott's apartment upstairs in the funeral home. Paige had driven up the road to the Great Machipongo Clam Shack and had brought home some fried oysters, crab cakes, hush puppies and a quart of she-crab soup. Nott was drinking a Smith Island Stout, and Paige was sipping a Church Creek Chardonnay. They were quiet as they enjoyed the wonderful food.

"Do you want some coffee with dessert?" asked Paige.

"Dessert? I'm as full as a tick now."

"Well, I stopped at Little Italy in Nassawadox on the way back and picked up some tiramisu, but if you're too full..."

"Whoa! Bring it on."

Paige smiled indulgently.

After supper, they sat at the table continuing to worry the situation like a hound with a bone.

"Nott, I think we need ... well, you need to go back to some of the other camps and ask around. See if anyone has noticed any strangers in the camps, other than you, that is."

Nott nodded in agreement. "And maybe you can talk with that Glorianna, again. Maybe she's got some more ideas."

Paige agreed. "We'll start first thing tomorrow."

The next morning Paige called Glorianna for an appointment and learned that she'd be making her rounds on The Shore. "Wonderful," said Paige. "I'd like to meet you at the camp in Capeville with Nott, and then I'll buy you lunch at the Mallard Cove Beach Bar."

"Now that sounds like a plan. I can meet you at the camp around ten, okay?"

"See you then," Paige replied, excited to be getting back in the hunt.

Paige and Nott pulled onto the dusty main road of the Carpenter Camp in Capeville just before ten o'clock. It was a work day, so the camp was largely deserted, with just a few toddlers, too young to pick, and their mothers around.

"Hey Paige, Nott," said Glorianna as they got out of Paige's car.

"Whew," said Paige. "Hot enough for you?" Then she snorted. "That was pretty lame, wasn't it?"

Glorianna snorted herself. "Well…"

The moved into the shade. "What can I help you with, Paige?"

"I'm still hung up on trying to find out what happened to little Claudita Briones. Deputy Pablo is just going through the motions, Sergeant Heath says it's not in his jurisdiction, and I'm afraid that she's just going to be forgotten and buried in a pauper's grave with no closure on who did it. We even went across and talked with the FBI, but they weren't real helpful, either."

Glorianna nodded her head sympathetically. "Yes, and like I said before, she's not the only one."

"You said that. That's terrible. Their poor mothers must be frantic."

"Those that are still around."

"Yeah," said Nott, "you mentioned that some of them had taken off. Why's that?"

"They're Mexicans and they're illegal. Back home if they got caught doing something illegal the *policía* can be rough. The legal penalties actually aren't bad, but the *policía* will often charge huge bribes to let people go free. They're afraid that the police here will be just as corrupt. So they don't report crimes because they don't want to be noticed by the authorities, and in this case, when their daughters have gone missing, they are afraid the authorities will hear and come after them."

"Damn," said Nott. "I'm no fan of the cops, but I'm sure not afraid of them like that. Mostly, don't mess with them and they won't mess with you."

"You know that, and I know that," said Glorianna, "but these folks don't know that. And, too, back home it can be the *policía* who are responsible for people disappearing. They just believe they don't have anyone on their side. So, they split."

"Can we talk to some of the mothers who are here, now?" asked Paige.

"I'm not sure they'll want to talk. But let's try. Come on."

The three of them walked down the dusty road to one of the shacks. There was a smell of fried food, spoiled milk, and overripe garbage in the air.

Knocking on the door, Glorianna called out in Spanish, "Maria! It is I, Glorianna. I have two friends with me. May we come in and talk for a while?"

The door opened and a small skinny black-haired woman peered out. On her hip, she carried a baby who looked to be about 18 months old, and another little boy, maybe two years old, peeked shyly from behind her apron.

"Please, come in," she said softly.

As they entered and looked around, Maria waved to them to sit at the table in the kitchen. "I'm afraid I can't offer you much. Some lemonade?"

Glorianna shook her head. "No, *gracias* Maria." Then motioning to Paige and Nott she explained, "These two are the ones who found little Claudita Briones."

Maria quickly crossed herself

"They are very upset about what happened to the little girl. They are trying to find out who did it. I told them that other girls have gone missing also, and they are very concerned about them. And their *madres*."

Maria pulled her children closer to her as she nodded her understanding.

"Maria, have you any idea what has happened to these little girls?"

"No." She shook her head regretfully.

Paige spoke up. "Ask her if she has seen any strangers hanging around the camp."

"No," came back the answer. "Oh, some of the local boys come and try to flirt with some of the older girls. But the fathers deal with that quickly. They chase them away. Sometimes we will have a dance, and some of the local boys come and dance with our girls. As long as they behave, that's fine."

Paige nodded her understanding.

"But they are not really strangers," Maria said. "They are just local boys. From the high school."

"How about the law?" asked Nott. "Do they ever come into the camp and harass people?"

"No, the laws keep away. We have our own law. We have camp rules and we have common decency and they keep things okay. No need for the laws to come in and bother us simple people."

"How about the INS, the immigration people?" asked Glorianna.

"No," said Maria, "we don't usually see them in the camp." She thought for a moment. "We do see them out of the camp, though."

Nott asked, "What do you mean 'out of the camp'?"

"Well, sometimes we will see them driving by in a police car."

"A 'police car'?"

"Yes. It will be a police car with one man in it. You can see the 'INS' on his cap. That means Immigration Service, doesn't it?"

"Yeah," said Nott. "Immigration and Naturalization Service."

"Sometimes we see him in the store when we go in, in J.B. White's or B&B grocery. He has on the cap and a jacket that has those letters on the back—INS."

"Is he in uniform?"

"Oh, yes," said Maria. "A big man in a brown uniform with a gun and everything. And the cap and jacket with INS on them. Sometimes he, that man, will talk with some of the young girls. But we have told them all to stay away from him. That he will take them, and lock them up for being illegal, and send them back to Mexico without us, their parents."

"Did you know any of the girls that have vanished?" asked Paige.

"I knew one. Maritza. She was a beautiful little girl. Very playful. She was a good learner, too."

"What happened?" asked Glorianna.

"We don't know. One evening she went up to the store for an ice cream. It was terribly hot. You know how it can get here. She went for an ice cream and never came back. We looked everywhere for her. We thought maybe she had been hit by a car, so we looked in all the fields and ditches by the road. Nothing.

She hugged her baby tighter, a shiver running down her spine. "We asked the man at the store. He said that she had been there and bought her ice cream, but that was all he knew."

"Was she alone at the store?"

"Yes. It was just her. We looked in the woods and in the fields but found nothing.

"Her mother was frantic. Her father, though, was very quiet. I think that he had been afraid something like this would happen. She was just so pretty and not afraid of anything."

Her eyes grew wide. She lowered her voice as if afraid the evil creatures might hear her. "Back home they would have said that the Chupacabra had got her. Here … I just don't know."

They sat in silence, thinking about what Maria had told them.

"Please, I am sorry, but I must feed the baby," said Maria, subtly suggesting they leave.

"Of course," said Glorianna. "I am sorry that we stayed so long. Thank you, Maria. You have been very helpful."

Nott and Paige nodded their appreciation and their farewell as they went back out into the street and then to their cars.

Glorianna followed them as they drove to the Mallard Cove Beach Bar. They got a table where they could gaze out the window at the few non-charter boats moored there. Pablo's bright yellow Cigarette boat was moored to one of the floating piers. There were a few sailboats, and off to one side, a magnificent vintage restored forty-two-foot Chris Craft named *Why Knot* which was the home of the marina operator, Marlin Denton, and his fiancée, Kari.

"What do you think?" asked Nott.

Paige shook her head. "I just don't know. It doesn't make sense to me. If these girls were killed, like little Claudita, why haven't their bodies shown up? And if they weren't killed, where are they?"

Nott added, "And if it was a sex-thing, then Claudita would have been ... uh, violated. Right?"

Paige looked at Glorianna. "Any thoughts?"

"It's enough to make me almost lose my appetite. Not quite, though. But no, I just haven't any idea at all."

"I guess I'll get back with Special Agent Hannegan at the FBI," said Paige. "I'll tell him what we've got so far and see if he can make any sense out of it. I'll call him after lunch."

The lunch was excellent, but the silence hung heavily over them as they pondered what to do next.

Chapter Twenty-Four

AS LUCK WOULD have it Special Agent Tim Hannegan was part of the Child Exploitation and Human Trafficking Task Force of the Federal Bureau of Investigation. As one of seven children, four of them girls, he had a deep belief in the protection of children, and in the Tidewater Area worked closely with the National Center for Missing and Exploited Children as they tried to stem the flow of children being sold for sex.

One of his main targets was the MS-13 operating in Norfolk. The MS-13 girls would approach their friends in high school and ask if the friend wanted to make some easy money. All they'd have to do was go on some dates with some older men. Once they agreed, they were trapped. The MS-13 members would hook them on drugs and keep them as sex slaves, to be used by patrons and members alike. It was lucrative for the gang because, unlike regular prostitutes and their pimps, the gang gave nothing to the girls but the drugs that kept them compliant.

Occasionally they'd snag a really elegant white girl. Then they would sell her to gangs who were running truck stop prostitutes along Interstate 20, known as the Sex Superhighway, in South Carolina. According to statistics from the Bureau's Task Force, in 2013 four times the amount of people were sold as slaves in America than the year before the Civil War, and usually for sex.

Girls that they ran themselves they would work until they began to get a bit shopworn. Then they'd sell them to gangs in Baltimore where they'd be put to work in the seedier areas of East Baltimore Street known as The Block. By the time the girls got there, they were no longer persons—they were merely receptacles. Ultimately, they would eventually be given a "hot shot," a lethal injection of heroin, and dumped in an alley.

When he received the call from Paige he had just been trying to track a fifteen-year old girl who had just gone missing from the Great Neck Middle School in Virginia Beach. He had been dealing with the frantic but belligerent parents and was very relieved at the prospect of a visit from the Eastville Coroner, as he thought of her.

It was late afternoon when Paige arrived at Hannegan's Chesapeake office.

"I'm really sorry to get here so late. I never considered that the 20-or-so miles would take me so long. I guess I'm just preoccupied."

"With what?" Hannegan asked.

"You remember I told you about that little girl's body we found trussed up in the creek?"

"The little Hispanic girl? Yes."

"It turns out that she isn't the only one."

"You've found more bodies?"

Paige shook her head. "No. I'm sorry. I mean we've found more girls that have disappeared. Gone missing."

"Tell me."

"Nott and I went with a lady from the Presbyterian Labor Ministry to another of the labor camps and talked with a woman who told us that there were at least two additional girls gone missing this year."

"Okay."

"They apparently went out to the store, for ice cream or something, and never came back. The people at the stores say that they were there, but they don't have any idea where they went after leaving."

"Could they have been in an accident or gotten hurt somehow? Did you check the hospitals?"

Paige shook her head again. "They looked in all of the fields and ditches and woods. Nothing. No one's seen them. They're just gone."

"Well, what can I do for you?"

"I don't know," Paige lamented. "No one on The Shore seems to have any ideas. The law isn't involved with these missing girls 'cause they were never reported…"

"Illegals?"

"Yeah, I think so. But they all sound the same. Undocumented farm workers, girls, young, pretty, and vanishing without a trace. Except for little Claudita."

"Claudita?"

"Yes, the little girl whose body we found.

"I was just hoping that you might have an idea about what we can do next. I'm at my wit's end."

"Well, first off, would you like to go out and get a bite to eat? My treat," said Hannegan.

"You know, that'd be nice," said Paige. *A dinner date with a handsome FBI Special Agent,* she thought. *Wowzers!*

"Come on. We'll take my car."

Hannegan drove them to a steakhouse called The Butcher's Son near Battlefield Boulevard.

"This isn't too fancy a place, is it?" asked Paige. "I'm really not dressed for it."

"No," he replied. "Just a kind of meat and potatoes place. I think you'll like it. I thought that a steakhouse would be a safer bet than seafood since you probably get enough of that over on The Shore."

Paige nodded.

The restaurant was crowded but they managed to get a seat in a back corner. The lighting was dim enough that Paige had trouble reading the menu.

"You want some wine?" asked Hannegan.

"No," answered Paige. "I've got to drive home tonight."

"Right."

They dined on New York strip steaks and baked potatoes and Paige declined any dessert. The restaurant was so noisy, though, that they weren't able to talk. Paige had kind of hoped to have some small talk, maybe even flirtatious, with the young Agent, but it just wasn't to be.

As they drove back to Hannegan's office, Paige once again asked what the Agent thought she should try next.

He sat quietly for a moment, maneuvering through the traffic, then said, "Paige, how many girls are missing?"

"At least three that we know of. Maybe more."

"All young girls?"

She nodded her head.

"I don't want to sound sexist, but were the girls ... cute? Attractive?"

"Agent Hannegan..."

"Will you please call me Tim?"

"Okay. Tim, what are you talking about?"

"Paige, I told you that I'm with the Trafficking Task Force. I'm just wondering if your missing girls were taken and forced into the trade."

"The trade?"

"Whether someone forced them to become prostitutes."

"Omigod, Tim! Please, no!"

Tim said, "Paige, the things I could tell you."

"Don't!"

"I won't, but the things the MS-13 is doing with their prostitutes..."

"MS-13? Aren't they the animals with the tattoos all over their faces and bodies?"

"Yeah, they are a gang from El Salvador. They're known for their high level of violence. And not just towards their victims. Any gang member who messes up stands to get their heads cut off, too."

A shiver of fear ran down Paige's spine.

"But ... but they couldn't go over to The Shore and pick these girls up. First off, with those tattoos any girl no matter how young would run at the first sight of them. And they'd stand out like a sore thumb on The Shore. There's just no way they could be over there hunting for little girls."

"No," said Tim, "but consider this: to the MS-13 these aren't 'little girls.' They're product. These guys have no common decency in them. Our little girls are just money-making products to them, like a rental car or something. They don't have any humanity, and they don't have any scruples. Buy 'em, use 'em, sell 'em. It's all just business."

"How horrible," said Paige.

"Yeah," said Tim. "And when one of them is pretty much used up, they'll just sell them up the road to the gangs in Baltimore, and then restock."

"Restock?"

"Get new girls. Get them, break them, hook them on drugs and put them to work on their backs."

"But we're talking babies," said Paige.

"Doesn't matter to them. They'll charge a premium for the new ones, the young ones."

"But how would the MS-13 in Norfolk be getting little migrant girls from the Eastern Shore?"

"That's what I've got to figure out."

Perplexed and alarmed, Paige drove back across the Bridge-Tunnel to the Eastern Shore. *My little girls,* she thought. *I've got to do something to protect these little girls. It wasn't so long ago that I was one of them. I've got to figure this out.*

Arriving at her apartment on Wilkin's Beach she poured herself a glass of Chatham's Merlot which she sipped in the shower. Then she fell into bed, only to have her sleep interrupted by recurring dreams of tattoo-faced men grabbing her and pulling her away to where she didn't know.

Chapter Twenty-Five

EARLY NEXT MORNING Paige drove up to Kate's Kupboard in Exmore for some sticky buns, and then stopped at Machipongo Trading Company for two cafes con leche. She unlocked the front door of the funeral home and climbed the stairs to Nott's apartment, calling ahead so he'd know she was on her way up.

As they sat at the table in his kitchen Paige told him what she had learned from Tim.

"Tim?" asked Nott.

"Yeah. He told me to call him 'Tim.' It doesn't mean anything."

Nott gave a half-smile.

"Tim thinks that the missing girls might have been taken by MS-13."

Nott's eyebrows raised in surprise. "Paige, you've lived here all your life. How would those tattoo-faced freaks get away with that over here? Everyone knows everyone. They could never get away with it."

Paige nodded silently and sipped her coffee. "I looked them up on the Internet, and they have a big presence in the Norfolk area. Nott, who else could it be?"

"Don't know."

"I'm going to get together with Pam and Donna and see what they think. You want to come along?"

Nott shook his head. "You go have your hen party. I'll stay here."

Donna's CBES office was in Eastville and Pam was the Eastville postmistress, so they decided to lunch at Yuk Yuk and Joe's and talk over what Tim had told her and what she had found from meeting with Glorianna.

Fortunately, the restaurant was not crowded, and they quickly found a table where they'd be able to talk. They all ordered soft crab sandwiches with sweet potato fries and water with lemon.

As they waited for their food Paige filled them in on what she and Nott had learned when they visited the Carpenter Camp in Capeville. She told them that there were at least two more girls missing. Maybe more.

"Why didn't we know anything about other girls?" asked Donna.

"They were never reported. The parents just don't trust the police. They didn't want to be noticed because they were illegals. Undocumented."

The other two nodded their heads.

Their food came, and they spent a few minutes getting arranged. Paige bowed her head and said a quick silent grace. So did Donna and Pam.

Pam took a bite of her sandwich and around the soft crab she asked, "What about Special Agent Dish? Have you talked to him?"

Paige smiled almost shyly remembering. "Actually, I had dinner with him last night across in Virginia Beach."

Donna's eyebrows went up. "Dinner? A date? Tell, tell." Pam almost choked on her fries.

"No, it wasn't a date. Although I guess I wouldn't have minded a date. No, I went over to tell him what I had found so far and see if he had any ideas."

"'Any ideas'," snorted Pam. "And *did* he have any ideas?"

Paige gave her a dirty look. "We were talking about our dead little girl and about the girls who are missing. It was business. That's it. I wish you'd go give your filthy mind a bath."

Pam wasn't contrite. "Well, I mean, you've got one man already living upstairs and now you're wooing another one across The Bay. I mean, *whoo whoo.*"

Donna reached over and smacked Pam on the shoulder. "Grow up, girl. I want to hear what happened."

"Like I said, we went out to dinner at a steakhouse, but it was too noisy to talk. So, we went back to his office and he told me about all of the prostitution that he's investigating."

"But doesn't prostitution involve older girls? Women? And aren't they, well, kind of in it for the money?"

"Honestly, Pam, I'd never really spent any time thinking about it," said Paige. "I mean, sure, I always knew it existed. But it's not the kind of thing nice people sit and contemplate, you know?"

Pam nodded thoughtfully.

"And Tim told me about this gang, the MS-13? You heard of them?"

Donna nodded her head solemnly. "I've read some stuff about them in the VIRGINIAN-PILOT. They're not nice, with all those tattoos. They had pictures. They even have tattoos all over their faces! And killing people. I mean, they actually cut people's heads off!" Paige nodded. "And the paper said that they are getting a real foothold in Norfolk, in the Grandy section. People are afraid to go out of their homes even in the daytime."

"Well, Tim says that they are deeply into prostitution. They have their female members befriend young girls at middle school or high school, promise them part-time work with easy money, and then when they've got them, they hop them up on drugs. They keep them high to control them."

Pam was now somber. "That's horrible," she said with a shudder. "Why don't the girls run away ... escape?"

"Tim says they can't. They keep the so hopped up on drugs that they're not capable of thinking. They keep them like that, then when they are finished with them, they either give them an overdose or sell them to gangs in Baltimore."

"Oh, dear Lord God," said Donna, tears starting to form in her eyes. "That's terrible. What can we do?"

Pam piped up, "Well they couldn't do that over here on The Shore. Have you seen pictures of those freaks? All the tattoos. Even on their faces! Over here they'd stand out like a marshmallow in a coal bin."

Paige agreed. "That's true. I don't see how they could be responsible for our missing girls. And they never would have been able to dump little Claudita in Cherrystone once they'd killed her."

The others nodded their heads.

They had finished their lunches and had to get back to work.

"What will you do now, Paige?" asked Donna.

"I think I'll try Pablo again," she replied. "Maybe he'll be interested in the possible gang connection."

"Well, good luck." And they parted.

Back in her office, Paige called Pablo and he answered on the fifth ring. "Hey, Paige. What's shakin'?"

"Pablo, I'd like to talk to you about Claudita and some other missing girls."

"Who?"

"Claudita. You know, the little girl whose body was found in Cherrystone Creek?"

"Oh, the one your live-in boyfriend killed."

Careful Paige. If you want his help you can't lower yourself to his sophomoric level.

Not responding to his taunt, she said, "I've talked with some folks down at the Carpenter Camp and it looks like there are more girls missing."

"Ain't no one filed any paper on it."

She kept on, "I'd like to see if you have any ideas. I talked to a Special Agent at the FBI, and – "

"YOU WHAT?" Pablo roared. "Don't you know that they ain't got anythin' to do with this? This is local jurisdiction. We don't need the damn F-B- f-ing-I coming in here, throwing their weight around and bogarting our case."

Paige was taken aback by his fury.

"Listen up, Paige. How about you and me go down to the Mallard Cove Restaurant for dinner tonight and we'll smooth all of this out. I gotta be down there workin' on my boat, anyhow, and maybe we can take a moonlight ride after we eat. How's that sound?"

After his outburst Paige wasn't sure, but she finally agreed.

"I'll be down there workin' on my boat. Whyn't you come on down 'round eight or eight-thirty, we'll eat, and I'll buy you some of that wine you like so much, and then we'll go cruising. Okay?"

Paige gave in. "Okay, Pablo. I'll see you tonight for supper. But I'm still going to want to talk about these missing girls."

"Yeah, okay. See you." And they disconnected.

Chapter Twenty-six

THE WEATHER WAS beautiful that evening as Paige drove down the highway to Mallard Cove. The occasional clouds that had been in the sky during the day had blown away, and the night was pinned with a million stars. Although she still missed Philadelphia sometimes, Paige had to admit that the City of Brotherly Love never had beautiful skies the way they did here on The Shore.

She pulled into the Mallard Cove Restaurant a little after eight and wandered down to the marina slips to find Pablo. She approached his sunflower-colored Cigarette boat that seemed to glow in the bright dock lights of the marina. The engine compartment was open, and she could see a greasy Pablo working down below.

"Pablo. Pablo!"

He stuck his head up from the engine compartment. "Hey, Paige," he called.

"Come on. You want to get some supper? It's late and I'm hungry."

"Okay. Wait until I go below and clean up," he said, as he wiped the grease off his hands with a shop rag and went down through the hatch to the Cigarette's small cabin. Paige waited on the dock.

"Pablo," she called, "I'm going on up to the restaurant. You come on up once you're cleaned up."

When she looked around while entering the restaurant she saw Sergeant Heath sitting by himself just finishing his dessert. She walked over to greet him.

"Hey, Sergeant! How're you doing?"

"Miss Paige. I'm doing just fine." He looked around. "You here alone?"

"No Pablo's been working on his boat. I'm waiting for him to clean up and come on up for supper." She paused, tucking a loose strand of hair behind her ear.

"Sergeant, have you heard anything more about that little girl's whose body we found?"

Heath shook his head. "No, ma'am. Ain't heard nothing. Guess we'll never know for sure."

"Did you know that there are other girls missing, too?" Paige asked.

"Well, I'd heard something about that, 'bout you askin' 'round."

"And?" she asked pointedly.

"Well, Paige, if there ain't no paper on them, there's nothin' I can do. Ain't no one filed a missing person, so I got no jurisdiction. Without official paperwork it's just hearsay, and the City Council don't pay me to go off on wild goose chases. What about the Sheriff's office—Pablo?"

"I'm going to talk with him more about it at supper, but so far he hasn't been very interested either. How can one little girl be killed, murdered, and several others disappear without a trace, and law enforcement doesn't care?"

"Now, Miss Paige, you know we care. But there are rules and protocols we gotta follow. You can understand that."

Paige snorted in anger and flounced off to her own table where she ordered a vodka and cranberry juice with a double shot of vodka. Wine wasn't going to make it tonight. She was too angry.

When Pablo came in Paige was on her second drink. Waiting a half hour for Pablo hadn't improved her attitude. But she wasn't a liquor drinker, and on an empty stomach, she was beginning to feel effects of the alcohol.

Pablo sat down, motioned to the waitress to bring him a beer and pointing to Paige's drink he circled his finger to indicate that she should bring Paige another. Paige tried to object, but Pablo ignored her.

"Why are you law-enforcement-types just ignoring this problem?" Paige said. "You don't care about the dead little girl, and I just talked to Heath and he doesn't care about the dead little girl. And the other little girls are missing, but you don't care about them either. I just don't understand." Her voice was rising.

"Shh, Paige," said Pablo. "People are starting to look."

"Don't shush me, Pablo. You guys are supposed to be sworn to take care of the public … the little guys. But here are these little girls, and you don't do nothing … anything. What's that all about?"

"Paige, like I told you before if no one has filed a complaint, or a missing person report, our hands are tied."

"Well, what about little Claudita?"

"Okay, yeah, having a dead body makes it official, but no one is looking for her. It took you forever just to find out her name, but you never were able to find her people. And I've got other cases that I've got to work on … cases where people, prominent citizens, are expecting action. She's just a little Mex girl that no one is looking for, so it's way down the list of things to do."

"'Just a little Mex girl.' And what are you, Scandinavian? With a name like 'Pablo'?"

"Paige, you know my people were from El Salvador, not Mexico. And we weren't migrant farmworkers. So, there's no comparison."

Paige was starting to get loud, again, so Pablo called the waitress over and ordered some dinner to go. "Come on, Paige. You're drunk. Let's go down to my boat and you can sit down, and we can eat in peace."

Grumbling, Paige got to her feet and allowed Pablo to guide her through the tables of the restaurant, out into the night and down to where his boat was moored. "Besides," said Pablo, "it's a beautiful night out. We can sit in the cockpit and enjoy the stars while we eat."

They sat in the sumptuous seats of the boat's cockpit and ate their clam fritter supper making small talk.

"Thirsty?" asked Pablo?

"Yeah," said Paige. "Just nothing alcoholic. I think I've had enough for one night."

Laughing Pablo went below into the cabin and returned with a bottle of water for Paige and a Cobb Island IPA for himself. "You sure you don't want a beer?" he asked as he raised his dripping green-and-white can.

Paige shuddered, and Pablo chuckled. "I'm not trying to get you drunk so I can have my way with you. You've already got yourself drunk."

Paige sipped at her water. "I don't want you to take this the wrong way, but I think I need to lie down."

"Sure," he replied. "Let me help you down into the cabin. It ain't fancy, but those leather benches are real comfortable."

Weaving just a bit, Paige allowed Pablo to take her arm and ease down the couple of stairs into the cabin of the Cigarette boat. Although it wasn't as fancy as a cruiser might be, the cabin still smelled of fine leather, and the benches with the CIGARETTE logo embroidered into their leather backs were soft. She sat down on the starboard bench and Pablo sat to port across from her.

Perhaps seeing the cabin of the boat for the first time through a haze of alcohol Paige could see why Pablo was so proud of his boat. "This is really nice, down here," she said. "'Course you couldn't actually *live* here, but it's real nice."

Pablo beamed. "Yup, prettiest and fastest boat for its class on The Bay. I told you it'll do close to eighty, didn't I?"

"Yeah. I think we've about done that when we've been out riding." She ran an appreciative hand over the smooth leather.

"It's sure pretty. How much does a boat like this cost?"

"Ooo, a lot of money. New, with all the bells and whistles, it'll set you back, oh, a half-mil."

"Half a million dollars?"

"Oh, yeah. But I got this at an auction the Feds were having. It was a drug boat that got seized, and I got a good deal. Actually," he said conspiratorially, "I knew a guy where they do the auction and he let me put in a bid on it before the public got a chance. I got a real good deal."

"But … even so. Where did you get that much money?"

"Well…"

"And doesn't it cost a fortune in gas? I remember Hop Hopkins, when I was a little girl, once telling me that on his Owens cabin cruiser, the Wild Rose, when he had it opened up, both engines took a stream of gasoline as big around as your little finger. He owned the Chevy dealership. I think he said he had twin 409-engines in there. He liked to say that he never burned much gas … in one spot."

Pablo's speech stumbled a little. "Well, yeah, it does drink the gas when you've got it wide open. But it's a lot better when you're just cruising or at a fast idle."

Paige half laughed. "When was the last time you took this boat out at a 'fast idle'? The only thing you know is balls-to-the-wall. Whoops! I must've had too much to drink to talk like that.

"But seriously, Pablo, how can you afford a boat like this on a deputy sheriff's salary?" She whispered, "You on the take?" and snickered.

"That's not funny, Paige," he said heatedly.

Paige stood up. "I gotta go."

Pablo stood, blocking her way to the hatchway. "You can't go; you're too drunk to drive." He laughed. "I'd have to arrest you for DUI."

Paige tried to push past him. "I gotta go," she said more forcefully.

"No, Paige. Come on, why don't you just sleep it off right here?" He moved to take her in his arms. "I can make you comfortable and help you relax, and I'll stay right here to protect you." He tried to kiss her while his hands were busy groping her.

"Stop it," Paige shouted, struggling against him.

Pablo just laughed. "C'mon, Paige, you know you want this. Why else did you fortify yourself with booze then let me bring you down here?" His hands began to tug at her trouser belt.

"Stop it," Paige bellowed. She pushed against him so hard that she, herself, was the one sent flying, and she ended up on the floor of the cabin with the bench cushion pulled down on top of her. And there was something else. Hidden under the cushion was a jacket emblazoned with INS FEDERAL AGENT across the back, and a ball cap with INS in big letters above the brim.

Paige took them in her hand and looked blearily at them. She stood facing Pablo. "What on earth are these? Pablo, why do you have Immigration Service stuff?"

Again, she tried to push past him to the hatchway, but this time Pablo backhanded her hard enough to knock her down again.

"You're the one, aren't you?" she whispered breathlessly. The side of her face where Pablo had hit her was hurting and beginning to swell up, but she wasn't sure whether the tears in her eyes were from the pain or the dawning realization about Pablo.

"You pretended to be an INS agent in order to snatch those little girls," she accused.

Pablo just stood there.

"Why, Pablo? Did you kill the others too?"

Pablo shook his head. "Dammit, Paige. You're spoiling everything. No, that one was a mistake. The others were too scared of me to do anything, but that one –"

"Claudita?"

"She started to try to get out of my patrol car. When I reached over to grab her she bit me. She bit me! Hard. Drew blood! Then she started to scream. I spun her around and put a choke hold on her. You know, just to quiet her down. Used to use them all the time in the Corps. Little choke and bingo, out like a light. I just wanted to shut her up."

"But you killed her."

Pablo dumbly nodded his head. "Yeah. I guess I was too mad from her biting me and I guess I held it too long. Normally it's just a couple of seconds and the perp is out for a while."

"But?"

"But when I let her go, she wasn't breathing."

"She was dead. You killed that little girl. So, you put her in Cherrystone Creek."

"What else could I do? I got some old fishing pound net and wrapped her up and weighted it down with some chunks of cement. I put her on the bow of my kayak so that I could get up into the shallow water, and put her in. I figured the crabs would take care of the body for me. Lost a lot of money with that one, though."

"Wha'd'ya mean?"

"I've got a standing order with my old buddies in MS-13 over to Norfolk. They'll buy every virgin little girl I can get them. I just wait 'til I see a pretty little girl by herself, pull over and tell her I'm with INS and I'm taking her to the main office in Norfolk. Then drive her across The Bay and give her to my homeboys. They pay good. How do you think I can afford this boat?" He smiled, self-satisfied.

Paige just sat there appalled. He was actually proud of his business. She couldn't understand it. It was just like Special Agent Hannegan had said.

Hannegan! Paige had to let Hannegan know what she had found out.

She was still a bit dizzy, from the booze or the hit to the face she didn't know which, but she still struggled to her feet and headed for the hatch.

"Where do you think you're going?" asked Pablo.

"I'm sick," she said. "The booze and ... I'm gonna puke. Let me outta here!"

"So you can call your precious FBI guy?" He grabbed her roughly by the arm. "You aren't going anywhere. You're pretty old, but maybe my guys across The Bay will give me something for you. At the very least, they'll know how to make you disappear. 'Specially when I tell them how you want to pull this all down around us."

Paige wasn't a big girl, but fear gave her strength as she struggled in Pablo's grasp. Violently he spun her around and began to position her for a choke hold. Paige reached down between his legs and grabbed. And twisted. And dug her fingers, made strong from her work, into Pablo's most tender area. He pushed her away and as he did she spun and venting all of her fear and frustration delivered an award-winning place kick right into his ... place. Pablo's face went gray and he sank to his knees.

Finally making the hatchway, Paige sprang into the cockpit of the boat and began yelling for help. As she yelled she clambered up onto the dock and began running for the Beach Bar. The bar patrons heard her coming and her cries for help and poured out to see what was happening.

She was gasping for air as she reached the safety of the crowd. They could see her bruised face and asked what had happened.

Just as she started to explain she heard a deep guttural growl from the dock. Pablo had come up from below decks, started the Cigarette boat's twin Mercury 565 horsepower engines, and was getting ready to run for it.

"Stop him," she said pointing at the bright yellow boat that had just slipped its moorings and was headed for open water. "He's the one that killed the little girl." She looked around and saw Sergeant Heath. "Heath! It was Pablo. He killed the little girl and stole the other missing girls. Stop him!"

Sergeant Heath took out his phone and quickly called the Coast Guard Station in Cape Charles. He didn't have anything that could catch Pablo's boat. For that matter neither did Station Cape Charles, but the Coasties had radios and they had helicopters. They'd get him.

One of the charter boat captains, Bill Cooper of the *Golden Dolphin*, came over to her. "What's all the commotion?"

"The guy that just left here in the Cigarette boat. He killed a little girl and kidnapped some others. We've got to stop him."

Cooper looked over at his friend "Spuds" O'Shea. "C'mon. We can't catch him, but maybe we can keep him in sight." They ran to the *Dolphin,* jumped on board, and motored out of the marina in pursuit. Before they could even clear the mouth of the marina they could hear the scream of the Mercuries as Pablo slammed his throttles forward.

Chapter Twenty-seven

PABLO DIDN'T REALLY have a plan for his escape, he just knew that he had to get away from Mallard Cove Marina, for that matter the whole Eastern Shore, just as quickly as he could. He was glad that he always topped up his fuel whenever he returned to the dock, so he could run wide open and far.

As he raced up The Bay the wind of his passing forced his face into an almost rictus grin. It was a shame this was over, but he knew he'd be able to relocate and get into something new. He'd reinvented himself before. And he was certain that his gang brothers in MS-13 would help him out, especially after all of the money he had made for them. How many girls had he provided them for their prostitution and trafficking business? Over the years it must have been six or eight. And just that one little girl to spoil the whole thing.

He glanced back over his shoulder and saw the aging yellow-hulled fishing charter boat, *Golden Dolphin,* in pursuit.

They might as well chase me in a rowboat, he thought, and he eased his throttles. *I'll let them think they are catching up, then I'll blow them out of the water with my acceleration.*

ON BOARD THE *Golden Dolphin* "Baloney" Cooper was smugly having a ball. "Damn fool," said Baloney. "Thinks he's gonna play with us. Long's he sticks in The Bay I'll be able to follow him on my radar and tell the Coasties where to pick him up."

As the *Golden Dolphin* closed on the Cigarette boat Cooper turned a powerful spotlight on and locked the fast boat in its beam.

Laughing at the futility of the pursuit, Pablo made an obscene gesture at "Baloney," and again slammed his throttles to the stops. He knew that his speed could escape the *Golden Dolphin*, but he had something else in mind. He had suffered insults from those charter captains who thought that he and his fast boat didn't deserve to dock at the same marina as working boats, and now it was time for some payback.

He knew that when he was running fast, planing on the top of the water, his hull would run in less than thirty inches of water. His draft. He also knew that the draft of an old fishing charter boat like the *Golden Dolphin* would draw more like three feet. He'd draw them in and run them aground. If he was lucky, he'd ground them on an oyster bed and rip their bottom out.

Again, he retarded his throttles to let the other boat keep up, if not catch up. Then he started easing slowly in toward the beach. Intent on following the *Golden Dolphin* wasn't paying close attention to their depth meter and came on behind him. Watching behind, Pablo saw the larger fishing boat suddenly slew a bit to port and come to a sudden halt, its hull partially out of the water, grounded on a sandbar. He threw back his head and laughed.

Slowing again, Pablo this time circled back toward the *Golden Dolphin*. Seeing Captain Cooper watching him from the bridge and shaking his fist in his direction, Pablo waved a mocking salute to them and turned north once more. Again he opened his throttles.

"I wonder if that damn fool knows where he is," said Baloney to his mate. "Keep the spotlight on him."

The wind in his face was making Pablo's eyes tear, and the reflection of that damn spotlight on his windscreen and dashboard was blinding as well. He never saw what was coming as, at close to eighty miles per hour, he crashed his bright yellow Cigarette boat into one of the concrete ships sunk as breakwaters at the site of the old Kiptopeake ferry dock. The fireball, as his full gas tanks exploded, was spectacular.

Epilogue

THERE WASN'T MUCH of Pablo or his boat left for the authorities. The Coast Guard set up a safety zone while contractors soaked up the spilled oil and salvors picked over what they could find. Divers had gone down and hoisted the two Mercury racing engines onto barges, but the collision and explosion had damaged them severely. Perhaps they could be fixed.

Pablo, himself, was mostly recovered in little bits and pieces, those the crabs didn't get, the entirety of his remains placed in a child-sized body bag and taken to Paige's funeral home for an initial post. Cause of death was pretty evident.

Nott went back to his shack on Cherrystone Creek, but he did take some of the money the Veterans Administration had been sending him to fix the place up a little bit. He bought a table and a couple of chairs at the thrift store in Exmore, and he started eating the occasional breakfast with Paige and Donna at the Cape Charles Coffee House. He still preferred eating at

Rayfield's with Miss Birdie, but now he paid for his meals and always left her a nice tip.

Special Agent Hannegan kept in touch with Paige, and she'd take the occasional trip across The Bay to go out with him for a steak dinner. He wasn't able to stop the trafficking by MS-13, but at least he felt good that they had closed off one of the suppliers.

Finally, the strangest thing to come out of all this, happened when the Coast Guard was investigating the collision at the S.S. Edwin Thacher, the concrete ship that is the southernmost point of the Kiptopeake Breakwater. A couple of the Coast Guardsmen boarded the old derelict to explore and came upon the remains of a man. The remains were skeletal, and the clothing had mostly succumbed to the elements, and there was no identification to tell them who they had found. The only clue, which the Coast Guardsmen who were from New Jersey and Pennsylvania respectively did not understand the significance of, were on the skeleton's feet. On his feet, reasonably unaffected by the weather, were the white rubber boots of a waterman.

Dedication

This book is lovingly dedicated to Smith Beach and its people, and all the folks of The Eastern Shore of Virginia.

Disclaimer

TO BE READ
(though it does contain a spoiler)

AS MY BOOK progressed, I began to worry about how the folks on the Eastern Shore would take it. I'm kind of rough on some of my characters in general, and on the Northampton County Sheriff's Department—well at least one fictional deputy, in particular. Please note that the deputy in question is a "come here," not a "from here." Not only that, one bad deputy should not be construed as tainting the entire department. As for the generalizations made about the residents, PLEASE, this is fiction. It's not about anyone living on The Shore. I'm just trying to entertain.

If you are insulted by my book, I not only apologize but I ask you to write to me, tell me what upset you, and let me try to assuage your anger. Thank you and God bless!

Emma

Acknowledgements

I NEED TO thank Don Rich (the COASTAL ADVENTURE series) and Michael Reisig (the ROAD TO KEY WEST series), two of my favorite authors, who convinced me to keep writing. David Thatcher Wilson whose Demon Series book THE EXQUISITE CORPSE gave me my main character, Paige Reese, fully developed. Hayley Goffigon Smith, Donna E. Bozza, and Kim Smith, all of The Eastern Shore. Donna, I hope that you approve of how I included you in the book. Thanks, too, to the Citizens for a Better Eastern Shore (http://www.cbes.org/index.html), of which Donna is Executive Director, which is a real organization trying to maintain the quality of life on ESVA.

The Cape Charles Coffee House exists and is a delightful spot in downtown Cape Charles. They are in a beautifully restored bank building. You really should check out their website at https://www.capecharlescoffeehouse.com/).

On the highway across the street from the Barrier Island Center, is Machipongo Trading Company (http://www.esvamtc.com/), another wonderful spot for coffee, sandwiches, soups, and sundries.

And as improbable as it sounds, Yuk Yuk and Joe's is a popular watering hole in Eastville. Looks like a dive from the outside, but inside you'll find warm Shore courtesy and great fresh seafood.

I'd also like to give credit to DonRichBooks.com and Florida Refugee Press, LLC of the Coastal Adventure Series of books for use of Mallard Cove Marina™, The Cove Beach Bar™, and The Cove Restaurant™.

Finally, I'd like to offer an apology to my Eastern Shore brethren. For the sake of the story I had to take the occasional license with some of the facts. You'll catch them, though anyone not familiar with The Shore shouldn't even notice.

Learn more about Paige in THE EXQUISITE CORPSE, available on Amazon.

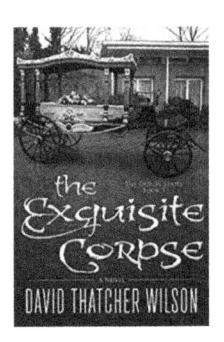

Made in the USA
Monee, IL
12 November 2023